OUR HOUSE

T. S. EASTON

Piccadilly
PRESS

First published in Great Britain in 2016 by
PICCADILLY PRESS
80–81 Wimpole St, London W1G 9RE
www.piccadillypress.co.uk

A CIP catalogue record for this book is
available from the British Library.

ISBN: 978-1-848-12567-4
also available as an ebook

1 3 5 7 9 10 8 6 4 2

Typeset in Sabon 14pt Extended by
Palimpsest Book Production Ltd, Falkirk, Stirlingshire

Printed and bound by Clays Ltd, St Ives Plc

Piccadilly Press is an imprint of Bonnier Publishing Fiction,
a Bonnier Publishing company
www.bonnierpublishingfiction.co.uk
www.bonnierpublishing.co.uk

For my family

Part One

Front Door

I noticed something was odd when I felt a breeze in the hall. I stopped for a moment, confused, then looked towards Front Door. It was open. I could see the steps beyond, heading down to the overgrown front garden. I could see a patch of grey, cloudy sky beyond that and a small red car parked on the road outside our house.

As I stood, gaping, a puff of wind blew some leaves and a crisp packet into the hall; they came to rest on the mat.

'D-Daddy?' I called nervously. Then louder: 'Daddy!'

Daddy poked his head out of the kitchen. William D was right behind him, hitting Daddy on the bottom with a broken lightsaber.

'Yes, Chloe?'

I just pointed.

'Stop it, William D. What is it, darli—' Daddy stopped speaking as he noticed.

'Front Door,' he gasped. 'It's *open*. Front Door is OPEN!'

There was a moment of complete silence as the house heard Daddy's cry and stopped to take in this big news.

Then Daisy appeared from the dining room to see the marvel. Mummy came clattering down the stairs, panting. William D stuck his head between Daddy's legs to get a better view.

Then, as we watched, Front Door began slowly to swing shut.

'No!' Mummy cried.

'Run, Chloe,' Daddy shouted. 'You're closest!'

And I did run. I sprinted along the long hall towards the closing door. It was like an action scene from a film set in a temple with traps and sliding doors. Through the coats on the coat rack, leaping over a pile of shoes. Just as I swerved past the telephone table, I realised I wasn't going to make it. Front Door seemed to have noticed me coming and was swinging shut even faster.

'Dive, Chloe, dive!' Daddy screamed.

And I *did* dive. I leaped, I sprang, I crashed and I slid.

And just as Front Door was about to click shut, I hooked my fingers around the door jamb and held it. Front Door was still open.

The Deal family cheered. Except for Jacob because he wasn't there.

'You did it, Chloe!' Mummy said. 'You did it!'

I was a bit surprised. Usually I make a mess of things like this. I fall over a lot, I'm very clumsy. Mummy says it's like living in a Greek restaurant because I break a lot of plates. Today, though, I'd stepped up, risen to the challenge and totally nailed it!

'Right,' Daddy said. 'You stay there and keep it open while we finish breakfast.'

It was a bit chilly on the steps. It's been rotten weather for June and May was miserable too. Daddy says we usually have Sandwich Summers in England, where you have nice weather at the start and nice weather at the end and something horrible in between.

'That doesn't sound like a very good sandwich,' Daisy had said.

'A dog poo sandwich,' William D had remarked, before laughing so much he fell off his chair.

'All the time!' Mummy said to him, exasperated. 'You just talk about poo ALL . . . the . . . TIME!'

I'm hoping this is a reverse-sandwich summer where you have nice weather in the school holidays, because we're going camping with our cousins, the Coopers. Also my birthday is coming up, on the same weekend school breaks up. I really want to have a big party in the garden but I'm not sure if that's going to happen. Mummy says the house isn't in a 'fit state' to receive visitors.

We've been living in our new house for nearly two years now. William D, who was four when we moved, can't remember the old house in the city. Daisy, who was only six then, says she can, but I know she gets things muddled sometimes.

I was eight when we moved and can definitely remember our old house. It had a tiny garden with no lawn. Now our garden is so big and overgrown Daddy can't find the mower he bought because it's lost in the long grass. The old house didn't have enough bedrooms for us all but the new house has so many bedrooms that William D can't remember which one is his. Our old house had noisy neighbours – now *we* are the noisy neighbours. Grumpy Mr Coleman from next door keeps popping his head over the fence to tell us to keep the volume down when we're playing Skink Hunt in the garden.

There were some things I didn't like about our new house when we moved. Some of the rooms have big damp patches with old wallpaper that is coming off and flaps in your face as you walk to the loo in the dark. The floorboards are creaky, with sticky-out nails, and the electrics need fixing. Sometimes Daddy gets a shock when he turns on the light in the hallway.

One thing that I really don't like about the new house, though, is the front door. Daddy says it has a mind of its own and he named it 'Front Door', with capital letters. He said Front Door was a she but then Mummy gave him a look and he stopped talking for a bit. Front Door doesn't open when you want it to. Sometimes it doesn't open at all, and at other times it suddenly swings open by itself. One night I heard a noise and came downstairs to find Front Door wide open and a little fox sitting on the hall mat staring at me. We stayed there for ages, just looking at each other in the moonlight, until the fox decided it was time to go. I wondered if it was a dream the next morning but then we discovered it had left a little poo on the steps as a reminder. William D stepped in it.

Front Door is especially tricky when there's wet weather. And that's why I had been so surprised to see Front Door open today. It had poured down overnight. I'd woken in the night and listened to the lovely sound of raindrops plopping against my little window at the top of the house. I'd snuggled up tight under the covers and tried to stay awake, just to enjoy the noise. And now here was Front Door, wide open – it seemed too good to be true.

Mummy and Daddy keep saying they are going to do something about Front Door but they never have enough money to get a carpenter out. That's another thing I don't like about the new house. We never seem to have any money here. Mummy and Daddy spent it all on buying the house and there is hardly anything left for buying things to put *in* the house. Anyway, that's why I'm not sure I'll be able to have a party. The house is in a state and there's not much money for things like that. Mummy says, 'We can't invite anyone around until I'm sure they'll actually be able to get into the house.'

One day when Mummy was away visiting Granny Jean and Daddy was in charge, he decided he was going to 'sort out Front Door once and for all'. He took us all to Home 'n Garden Megastore and bought an orbital grinder, some sandpaper discs to fit on it and a long length of metal chain. He also bought a short length of white plastic chain. He didn't want the white plastic chain but we had to buy it because William D was messing about and snapped it off the reel by accident and there was a man wearing a Home 'n Garden Megastore jumper watching us. There's usually someone watching when we go into shops with William D.

'Awkward,' William D had said. He says 'Awkward' a lot in an American accent. We have a pile of old Hannah Montana DVDs that he really likes to watch and I think he gets it from there. He also does the 'Loser' thing where you make an L sign on your forehead but he always uses the wrong hand and does it backwards. Mummy says 'Awkward' is William D's catchphrase. But he doesn't always say it at the right times because he doesn't really know what it means. On this occasion he got it right because it was a little awkward with the man in the Home 'n Garden Megastore jumper watching us. While we were there, Daddy also bought some tester pots of paint. We have a lot of paint tester pots because Mummy can never decide exactly what colour she's going to paint the sitting room. Daisy and I are always allowed to choose one each to take home, and Daddy chooses all the creamy, wheaty, nearly white, off-white sort of colours so Mummy can paint squares on the wall and stare at them for ages, turning lights on and off. Today he got Charleston Grey, Wimborne Matchstick and Hovis White.

Daisy always chooses lilac. She decided ages ago that it was the colour she wanted for her room so now she's painting her bedroom bit by bit with each tester pot from Home 'n Garden Megastore. We go there at least once a week, so she's already finished one complete wall and started on the bit around the window. On that particular occasion I chose Lemongrass Whisper, more for the sound of the name than the colour. It turned out to be a sort of mouldy green when I put it on the wall. I didn't like it. I'm not in a hurry to choose a colour for my bedroom walls because I like my room as it is, even though there's a patchwork of not-very-nice colours with silly names on one wall.

Anyway, when we got back home we sent Daisy through the rhododendron to the back door. She came through the house and opened the window in the front room and we all climbed in. Then we had one more try to open Front Door. So we all went back out through the window except William D who stood on a chair inside and turned the latch while the rest of us shoved as hard as we could from outside. It didn't work. Eventually Daisy slumped onto the doormat, panting.

'We'll never open it,' I told Daddy. 'Front Door knows you want to sand her so she'll never open up now.'

'We'll see about that,' Daddy said. He went back to the car and got the metal chain he'd bought. Then, with lots of 'oofs' and 'arghs' he crawled in through the front window again and into the hall. We all followed him, giggling. Daddy slid the iron bar through the last link in the chain, so that it looked like a strange sort of anchor. Then he poked the rest of the chain back through the letter box. Front Door wouldn't open (of course) so we climbed back through the front window, where Daddy picked up the chain from the steps and attached it to the back bumper of our car.

Daisy and I exchanged worried looks.

'What's he doing?' Daisy asked.

'He's going to use the car to pull the door open,' I said.

'Will that work?'

'I don't think so,' I said.

Daisy always thinks I know everything about everything. I do know quite a lot. Mrs Fuller says I'm very observant. When I told Mummy this she raised an eyebrow and pointed out that I never seem to observe when my room needs tidying. But that's not the sort of observing I mean. For instance, I really love nature documentaries and I'm always noticing wildlife in the garden or the park. I used to collect bugs and things in jars but they always died and so now I just watch them in their natural habitat, like the family of mice who live in William D's old welly boot.

I'm good at noticing things about people too. You can always tell what people are thinking by the way they move, or their expression, or how they pause before talking. Daddy says I'm *empathic*, which means you notice what other people are feeling. It took me a long time to realise that not everyone's like that. Some people don't care what other people are feeling or don't even realise that other people have feelings at all. And certain people know you have feelings and try on purpose to hurt them. People like Imogen Downing.

'Now,' Daddy said, coming back after starting the car. 'Two important safety tips for you all to remember: Safety Tip One is I want you all to go upstairs into the back bedroom, just in case the chain snaps. We don't want anyone sliced in half. OK?'

'OK,' I said. 'What's Safety Tip Two?'

'Safety Tip Two is don't tell your mother about this.'

'How is that a safety tip?' I asked.

'If she finds out what I've been up to, she'll kill me,' Daddy replied.

So we went back in through the window and upstairs but we didn't go to the back bedroom, of course. We went into Mummy and Daddy's room. William D was wearing a plastic policeman's helmet for protection. Daisy swallowed nervously as Daddy revved the engine. I remember thinking how lucky, or possibly unlucky, Daddy was that the car was parked outside the house today. Usually there isn't a parking spot nearby so we have to park way down the road, or sometimes even around the corner on St George's Road. With a big *vroom*, the car suddenly shot forward, pulling the chain tight. We heard the iron bar slam up against Front Door from the inside. But it wasn't Front Door that gave way. Nor did the chain snap. Instead, the whole bumper came off the back of our car with a *ping*, the chain whipped back and the whole thing shot in through the sitting room window, smashing a porcelain elephant on the shelf. The bumper ended up behind the sofa, all bent, and when Mummy got home, William D told her all about it before she'd even taken off her coat. Anyway. That was that. Front Door stayed shut when she wanted, and opened when she pleased.

So there I was, this morning, a wet Thursday in June, guarding our exit. Mummy brought me some cereal in a plastic bowl and I sat with my feet over the top step, watching the raindrops splash in a puddle that had formed in a crack in the paving stones at the bottom of the steps. Suddenly there was a black flash as something shot past me.

'Clematis!' I cried. The cat scuttled down the steps and stopped for a moment, blinking, before ducking under the rhododendron at the side of the house. The cat's real name is Sebastian, but when he was a kitten he just wouldn't stop climbing up the curtains, so Mummy called him Clematis, which is a type of climbing plant, and the name stuck.

We do have another cat, called Jeremy. He's a rescue cat. Daddy says he's not very bright, which I think is a mean thing to say about a cat. Mummy calls him The Slug, because he just lies around most of the time but also because he likes to eat slugs. He is disgusting. When we first got Clematis he brought in lots of animals from the garden and would drop them in front of us, looking pleased with himself. Mummy would grab us children and take us into another room while Daddy would have to deal with the bird, or the mouse, or the frog. We could usually hear him making gagging noises. I think that The Slug felt the whole hunting business was a bit too much effort. Why wait for ages, creeping about trying to catch something that moves quickly, when you can just wander out and get a slug? They must taste disgusting, but as Mummy pointed out, raw blackbirds are hardly a delicacy. The problem is, he ends up with sticky slug goo all around his mouth that doesn't come off for ages. He doesn't seem to mind.

I stood on the top step and looked down to the side, hoping Clematis had scurried through to the back garden. But then I saw him dart across the small front garden and spring up onto the brick wall. He peered over and looked interested, like he might jump down onto the pavement. I ran down the steps after him quietly so as not to scare him away and before Clematis realised what was happening, I grabbed him around his fat little waist. Luckily, Clematis is an affectionate cat. He loves people and is happy to be carried around by us, most of the time.

As I turned to take him back inside, I saw Front Door swinging shut.

Slam, went Front Door.

Click, went the lock.

'Bother,' went me.

Clematis wriggled free of my arms, dropped gracefully to the ground and ran through the rhododendron to the back garden. The rhododendron grows at the side of our house in the alley that takes you round to the back door and garden. It's a massive bush with thick branches spreading out all over the place so it's quite hard to squeeze past, even for William D. It has pretty purple flowers on it in spring but now it's just green, wet and in the way. The worst thing about Front Door sticking shut was that it meant we had to use the back door, which meant you had to push your way through the jungle at the side of the house, including the rhododendron. If it was dry, you ended up with twigs in your hair and leaves in your shoes. Mummy once said she found a squirrel in her handbag after going through the rhododendron.

And if it was wet like today? Well, you got completely soaked. Especially Mummy, who often turned up at school drop-off 'looking like a drowned rat' as she would say.

'Been at the gym?' the other mums would ask.

'Yes,' Mummy would reply. Even though technically this was a lie, I thought it was fair enough under the circumstances. Some of the other mummies at school drop-off look really pretty. They wear make-up and nice

14

shoes and have twig-free hair. I think Mummy is prettier than any of them but she's not at her best when she's been through the rhododendron.

So today Mummy would get wet again, and it was all my fault. I pushed my way into the giant bush, pulling a face as the cold, wet leaves dragged themselves across me. I came out the other side and caught a glimpse of my reflection in the side window. I looked like I'd just swum across the Amazon. After a quick check for leeches, I made my way to the back door and peered through the glass panel. They were all in there. Laughing. Mummy with her long dark hair and handsome Daddy in his blue shirt with the missing button. Silly William D doing his Mexican Dance. Sweet Daisy wearing her favourite pink hairband. Even teenage Jacob had emerged from his room and was eating toast, propped up against the Aga with a blank look on his face.

I sighed a deep sigh. It was time to own up about Front Door.

I pushed open the back door and everyone stopped laughing and looked at me. They all knew straight away what had happened. What I'd done. Daisy got up and rushed off down the hall to check Front Door. There was silence, except for the ticking clock on the wall. It's one of those backwards clocks where the numbers go in reverse. Today I wished time would go in reverse too, back to before I'd let Front Door shut. It's a rubbish clock, really. Only Jacob can tell the time on it. Speaking of Jacob, he took one look at my scratched face as I walked in the kitchen door and quickly disappeared. Jacob doesn't like confrontation.

'Front Door is shut!' Daisy yelled, helpfully.

'Oh dear,' Daddy said. 'Never mind.'

'No, never mind,' Mummy said, in a strangled sort of voice. She was pretending she wasn't upset but I could tell she was. And for a moment, just a moment, she looked really sad, like she used to sometimes when we still lived in London.

And it was all my fault.

School

Twenty minutes later we arrived at the school gates. Mummy always drops us off first then walks down into town with William D. After she leaves him at the infant school she goes to work. She's very busy, my mummy, always on the go. She's constantly getting phone calls or texts about who is picking up whose children today, and who's taking them to swimming or Brownies or football. She's very good at organising and always knows where to drop the cakes off at the coffee morning or who's going to run the BBQ at the school fair or a hundred other things. Some of the other mummies don't do very much. Mummy says they just go for coffee somewhere and gossip and moan about how much they have to do.

It took a while, but we all noticed Mummy smiled a lot more after she stopped working in London and suddenly she was there much more. When you needed her. Sometimes she says she'd like to go back to work as a lawyer just to get some rest but she's joking, I think. Now she works in town in an office, just part time, and though she sometimes moans about her boss, we can tell she's so much happier. Mummy is very funny, though sometimes she makes jokes I don't understand. Jacob says she's sarcastic. Daddy laughs at her jokes until he can't breathe. That's one of the things I like about her best, when she makes Daddy laugh until he can't breathe.

Mummy is one of those people who doesn't laugh very often herself. She's better at making other people laugh. Sometimes, late at night, if I can't sleep, I come out of my room and sit half way down the stairs. I can just see their heads through the open door to the TV room and they're watching some programme but not really watching it because they're chatting quietly. I can never hear what they're saying, just Daddy's deep grumble and Mummy's soft voice. Every now and again Mummy will say something that makes Daddy laugh so hard I think he's going to choke.

Sometimes, when they have a row, I worry that Mummy and Daddy might break up, like my friend Emily's parents did. But when I hear Mummy making Daddy laugh I stop worrying for a bit because how could Daddy leave someone who makes him laugh like that? And how could Mummy leave someone who thinks she is the funniest person who has ever lived?

My mummy is beautiful but today it had been a bad 'jungle run', as Mummy put it. The rhododendron seems bigger and thicker than ever, and every time you so much as touched a leaf, a shower of raindrops soaked you through. In preparation Mummy had changed out of her summer dress into some grey trousers and her old black cardigan.

As usual there was a cluster of mummies at the gates to Weyford Junior School. It was mostly mummies at school drop-off. There were a few daddies dropping off children too, sometimes wearing suits or paint-stained overalls but they didn't tend to hang around chatting. Usually my friend Emily from across the street walks with us but due to the Front Door disaster and Mummy having to get changed, we were late getting out of the house so Emily must have gone on ahead. I saw her mummy, Vicky, standing talking to Imogen Downing's mummy, Ellen.

Do you know how at school some girls are very popular and everyone wants to be their friend but secretly you don't really like them very much and they're a bit mean to you? Imogen is a bit like that, and so is her mummy.

Mummy tried to sneak past without us being seen but Ellen saw her.

'Polly!' she said loudly.

'Oh hello, Ellen,' Mummy said, rolling her eyes.

'Been for a swim?' Ellen asked.

'Um, no,' Mummy said.

'It's just that your hair is all . . .' Ellen stopped and reached towards Mummy, who flinched away but too late. Ellen pulled a twig from Mummy's hair and inspected it.

'Oh, that's where it went,' Mummy said, plucking it from Ellen's fingers.

'Is this a new look?' Ellen asked.

'Well, I've tried going through the hedge backwards,' Mummy said, 'and today I thought I'd go forwards instead.' She was making a joke out of it but I could tell she wasn't best pleased. She turned and kissed me on the cheek, then Daisy.

'Work hard today, girls,' she said. 'If they ask if you want to be a lawyer when you grow up, say no.'

'That handbag has lasted well, Polly,' I heard Ellen saying as we walked away. Poor Mummy. It was all my fault she was in such a state. As we went into the school, Imogen caught up with me. She had a loom-band bracelet on. Loom bands are so old-fashioned now.

'Your mummy had a twig in her hair,' she said, smirking.

'I know,' I said. I told her about the rhododendron, hoping she'd think it was funny.

'Why don't you get your gardener to cut it down?' Imogen asked.

'We don't have one,' I said. 'We just have Daddy, and he's not much good in the garden.'

It's sort of hard to explain to someone who doesn't know my daddy about what he's like. He's really clever and got amazing results at school and university, but he's only clever in a certain way. For example, Daddy works in IT but he can't fix the computer, or make the printer work, or programme the TV recorder box, or remember any passwords or do anything that might be helpful around the house. Sometimes he works from home. He analyses computer programmes for banks so his job is all about numbers, and spreadsheets with numbers on. Daddy's the opposite of me in that he's not very observant about people or events or jobs that need doing.

Imogen pulled a sniffy face when I explained about not having a gardener. 'We have a man who comes three times a week,' she replied. 'He's very good at topiary.'

'Daddy's good at spaghetti carbonara,' Daisy boasted.

'You'll be late for class,' I told her. She wasn't helping.

'OK,' Daisy said and ran off. She doesn't realise that Imogen is teasing us. Daisy's so lucky. She doesn't have any mean girls in her class. She's really popular and has loads of friends. Also, her teacher, Miss Jervis, plays the ukulele in class when she wants them to quieten down.

Unfortunately, Imogen is in my class. She was in my class in Year Four as well and will be in my class in Year Six, because that's the way they do things in this school. I asked Mummy if I could move to another class and she said she was sorry, but I needed to find ways of dealing with bullies.

'Were you ever bullied at school?' I asked Mummy one bedtime.

'Oh yes,' she said. 'Debbie Wilkinson flushed my Rick Astley pencil case down the loo once.'

'How did you cope with it?'

'Sarcasm,' she replied, with a cheeky grin.

21

'What's sarcasm?' I asked.

'It's when you say something you don't mean,' she said.

'Like when Daddy says he's going to mow the lawn?'

'No, that's called lying. Sarcasm is when you say something in a certain tone of voice that makes it clear you mean the opposite. Like "Thank you VERY much for standing on my foot, Chloe".'

I giggled. 'Or "Mummy, I'm SO happy it's raining on us".'

'That's it,' she said, smiling. Mummy is so pretty when she smiles. 'Or "I REALLY LOVE fighting my way through a rhododendron bush every morning".'

'Did sarcasm stop the bullies?' I asked.

'No, but it made me feel better,' she said.

As we neared the classroom Imogen saw Hannah and Sophie and ran off towards them without even saying goodbye. I used to be really good friends with Hannah but these days Imogen just acts as if she owns her and won't let anyone else be friends with her. As I passed them in the hall Imogen started whispering and I knew she was talking about me and my twiggy mummy. Luckily Emily was outside the classroom so I went and talked to her. I wish I was more like Daisy, with lots of friends. But when I think about going up to talk to other girls I get really nervous and worry that they're going to tease me. It's easier just to stay with Emily.

'What's wrong?' Emily said, seeing my face.

'Imogen,' I said. 'She's being mean again.'

'What did she say?'

That's the thing, it's hard to explain exactly what Imogen says that's so mean. I can tell she's mocking me, and it makes me feel sad and hurt. But to other people, it's just like she's making conversation. When I tell Daddy the sort of things she says, he always replies, 'That doesn't seem so bad. Maybe Imogen just isn't very good at expressing herself.' Mummy understands. She knows what girls can be like. But I try not to talk to Mummy about it too much because I know it upsets her.

'What can I do?' I asked Emily. 'If Imogen was pushing me, or putting chewing gum in my hair then I could show Mrs Fuller and she'd get in trouble, but she doesn't do anything obvious.'

'Why don't you use the sarcasm thing?' Emily suggested. I'd told Emily about sarcasm and we had agreed to try it out next time Imogen was being mean. Finally, here was my chance.

When Mrs Fuller opened the door we waited for Imogen's gang to move first and walk past us, and then Imogen gave me a sideways look and smirked again. Sarcasm time, I thought.

'I REALLY like your loom-band bracelet, Imogen,' I said as she walked by.

'Thanks,' she said, and carried on walking. Emily and I watched her go.

'Well, that didn't work,' Emily said.

* * *

Apart from Imogen annoying me, today was a good day at school. Daisy's teacher, Mrs Jervis, has started a ukulele club and lots of us went along at lunchtime and learned how to play 'My Dog Has Fleas'. Tobias broke three strings on his ukulele so Mrs Jervis gave him a tambourine instead until he pulled off one of the metal bits and swallowed it. Everybody laughed. Tobias can sometimes be a bit frustrating, but everyone knows he needs extra help with things and we all look after him.

After lunch we had English, which I was excited for because Mrs Fuller had already told us that were going to be given our creative writing project, to be handed in by the end of term. She handed out sheets to us all with the topic 'My House'.

She said we had to use our observational skills at home and write a paragraph or two about each room in our house. We had to describe the room and then say what usually happened in it.

'What, like "This is the kitchen where Mum cooks oven chips"?' Daniel asked without putting his hand up.

'I was hoping for a little more detail,' Mrs Fuller said, 'but yes, pretty much.'

I was a bit disappointed by this project. I'd been looking forward to having some creative writing to do because I love writing. But I thought it was going to be fiction. I wasn't at all sure about writing about my house. What could I say about it except that it was a mess and you couldn't open Front Door?

'It's going to take me ages,' Imogen said, just loud enough for me to hear. 'There are just so many rooms in my house.'

'Is there something you want to ask, Imogen?' Mrs Fuller asked.

'Oh yes, Miss,' Imogen said in her angel voice. 'What if you have two houses? We have a little cottage near Bournemouth.'

'Just your main house will do,' Mrs Fuller said, sighing a bit. I turned to see Imogen looking right at me with a smug smile. She is a real show-off.

'If you're writing about someone's bedroom, then say a few words about them too,' Mrs Fuller said. 'Or if your dad's always in the shed, then tell us about what he gets up to in there.'

Sleeping and listening to the Test Match is what my daddy usually does in the shed, I thought. Not very exciting. I might have to jazz it up a bit.

'Describe the things you like about each room,' Mrs Fuller said, 'and also the things you don't like. Now I'd like you to use some of the story-writing skills we've been working on this term, so watch your punctuation, your grammar and try to include some pieces of conversation using speech marks. Just little snippets here and there.'

I sat and thought about this. Mostly I like our new house, though I suppose it's not really all that new any more. But there are some bits that I don't like. I don't like the rhododendron, or the creaky floorboards on the first floor with the poking-up nails. I don't like the spare room, or the Megadeath room. The garden's great to explore, but sometimes I wish it was a bit tidier. Sometimes I remember our little house in London with its tiny garden that was just neat decking and a big flowery clematis. The rooms were small but properly decorated and full of pretty rugs and old furniture and lovely pictures. I decided to start on the project that night. Maybe I could make it interesting.

Daisy and I usually walk home with Emily's mummy, Vicky, and she gives us biscuits and we play until Mummy and William D turn up. Sometimes we go straight home when they arrive but sometimes Mummy sits with Vicky and they drink a glass of wine and talk about other mummies. Also sometimes our mummy tells Vicky what an awful time she has had at work. She really doesn't like her boss, Declan.

'Honestly, Vicky,' Mummy said tonight. 'Do you know he's suggested I do a Time Management course? He thinks the reason I'm always in a rush is because I don't know how to manage my time! The real reason is because he gets me to do all *his* work as well as my own.'

Emily's mummy is very good at dealing with my mummy when she's cross. She nods and tuts when she's supposed to and pours Mummy another glass of wine. Daddy isn't always quite so good at calming Mummy down – he makes mistakes, like interrupting Mummy when she's having a good old moan and telling her about *his* awful day instead.

'Oh yeah, you think that's bad?' he'll say. 'We go live on the new system in three weeks and I found out today half my team have been made redundant.'

Then he pours himself more wine without topping up Mummy's glass. Mummy doesn't say anything. She just looks thoughtfully out of the back window at the long grass.

Mummy's name is Polly and she used to be a lawyer in 'the City'. I remember when we lived in London and Mummy was still working in the City but I don't remember her being around all that much. She was just . . . well, not there. And very tired when she was around. Sometimes she used to fly to America or Geneva, which is in Switzerland, and she'd always bring us back Toblerones from Geneva because that's where they're from but then Jacob told me she didn't really bring them from Geneva but just got them from WH Smith at Gatwick.

After William D was born she went back to work but she hated it and would cry on Sunday evenings while we were trying to watch *Strictly*. One day she just got sick of it and told her boss she wasn't coming into work the next day. She and Daddy sold the house and we moved here. Jacob was cross because he had to change schools but Daisy and I were over the moon, especially when we saw the garden. Now Mummy's mostly much happier, but every now and then she still gets sad, like she used to in London.

Sometimes I want to shout at Daddy and explain to him exactly what he's doing wrong. Emily's daddy doesn't live with her mummy any more, and I sometimes wonder what it would be like if Daddy left us. But then when I think about it I can't imagine it. I think it's more likely that Mummy would leave. Sometimes I'm scared this will happen, sometimes when she's so cross she looks like she might explode. Or when she looks really sad.

Today she was more cross than sad, and William D wasn't helping. He's under a Dark Cloud at school. When I was at infant school, in London, we each had a peg with our name on. There were two rows of holes. One row was sunny and the other was cloudy. The teacher would move your peg to cloudy if you'd been naughty. I was usually on the sunny peg, but sometimes cloudy, usually when I was chatting when I shouldn't have been.

At William D's school, they have three rows. Sun, White Cloud and Dark Cloud. Jacob says they only introduced the Dark Cloud row when William D started. Mummy said that wasn't true but I could tell from the way she said it that she thought maybe it *might* have been true. William D is usually on White Cloud. Today he was on Dark Cloud because he'd eaten three crayons.

'One of them was black,' he told us at Vicky's house when we asked what had happened. 'There's only one black crayon and now it's in my tummy.' He didn't look guilty. He looked quite pleased with himself.

'But why did you eat it, William D?' Emily asked.

'Because William P wanted it when I'd finished with it and I didn't want him to have it,' William D explained.

'But once you ate it, you couldn't use it either,' Daisy pointed out.

'I didn't need to use it,' he said slowly, like he was talking to a baby. 'I'd finished with it.'

'That's very selfish,' I said. 'I think Mrs Duvall was right to put you under a black cloud.'

'You're poo!' he roared and ran off. He is SO naughty.

When we got home I sat down to work on my creative writing project. Writing about My House. Mummy let me use her computer, even though it's running slowly. I sat for ages, staring at a blank screen, trying to work out which room I should write about first. Eventually I decided to start at the top. In the room where I sleep.

My Room

Our house has four floors, not including the little pointy bit at the top which is the loft. There's the ground floor with the sitting room, the dining room (which is also the play room), the kitchen diner and a little bathroom. On the first floor are William D's room, Mummy and Daddy's room, the spare room and the big bathroom. On the second floor are Jacob's room, Daisy's room and the other bedroom which is supposed to be mine. But that's not my room, really.

When we first moved into our house, Mum and Dad put me in the attic room, 'just temporarily' while they decorated the bigger room for me on the second floor. But then the money ran out and they couldn't afford to do the decorating. Plus Daddy liked sitting in a deckchair in the garden reading a book more than scraping wallpaper so the room never was ready. Eventually Mummy asked me if I wanted to move into it anyway. We went to look at it again. The door had hardly been opened since we'd moved in and it groaned, like it was cross about being woken. The floorboards creaked under our feet as we walked in to the room. It felt cold and echo-ey.

Mummy said the room had nice high ceilings and a 'good aspect'.

She likes to watch programmes about people buying houses and doing lots of work on them to make them look different.

Daddy doesn't understand about wanting to change things. He says people should just find a nice house, move into it and leave it alone.

Mummy suggested we put my bed near the window, or near the radiator. It was one of those old-fashioned ones like you get in school, with thick pipes. I think it realised we were watching it because it gurgled at us. The radiators make a lot of noise in this house. Daisy says they talk to each other.

Everything in the house makes a noise. It's one of the things I like about it. Lying in my bed I can hear the groans of the timber in the attic, the low hum of the wind in the eaves, the creaks of people coming up and down the stairs, different pitches depending on which flight they're on. I can tell who's where just by the sound. Sometimes I think of all the sounds of the house being like an orchestra. Sometimes, all the instruments play together, in tune. Sometimes they don't. Just like the family.

So then Mummy asked me if I wanted to start moving my things in.

I was worried she might be cross if I said no, so I just said 'Um.'

We walked across the room to the window. There was a dead fly on the windowsill. I could see the garden down below with Daddy asleep on a deckchair, surrounded by long grass.

I must have looked glum because Mummy asked me what was wrong. I can't remember exactly how the conversation went, but it was something like this.

'I don't really want to move in to this room,' I said.

'Is it the mould?' Mummy asked.

'No,' I said.

'We'll paint over the Megadeath mural,' Mummy said. The estate agent who sold us the house told us this had been the room of the son of the lady we'd bought the house off. Megadeath is the name of a heavy metal band he'd liked. He's grown up now, though, and lives in Croydon so the Megadeath mural must have been there a long time. It covered an entire wall and showed a band of skeletons playing instruments on a battlefield.

'It's not that I don't like this room,' I said. 'Even with the Megadeath mural.'

'Then what is it?' Mummy asked.

'I just really like my room,' I said.

'This is your room,' she said, confused.

'No it isn't,' I said. 'My room is the one upstairs.'

'But it's so small,' Mummy said.

'That makes it cosy,' I said.

'And there's only one little window,' she pointed out.

'I like what you can see through it,' I said.

'And you can hear the bats,' Mummy said.

'I'm getting used to them,' I said.

Mummy leaned down and peered into my face which is a thing she does when she thinks you're not being truthful. I could hear William D shrieking in the garden.

'OK,' Mummy said, smiling. 'You are a silly sausage.'

I love my little room in the attic. Mummy says it was probably a servant's room back in Victorian times. If I wake in the night and can't go back to sleep I sometimes sit on the window seat and look out over the dark street. There are streetlights, but they're half obscured by trees in the summer so it all looks like a film set. The trees on the far side have blossom in the spring, the ones on this side go all different shades of red and gold in the autumn. There's always someone walking by, with a dog, or a shopping bag. Sometimes it's people I know and some of them, like Mrs Guptil, or Justin and Gavin from next-door-the-other-way, look up and wave to me.

So that's why I like my attic room so much. It is small and dark and you can hear the bats sometimes. But it's my room, and from there I can see everything that's going on in our street, our little corner of the world.

Batman

Just outside my attic room, there is a little flight of stairs that goes up to the loft. None of us are really sure what the difference is between an attic and a loft but that's what we call them. There are bats up there. They weren't there when we bought the house, but Daddy found them when he was up in the loft one day looking for a book. There are a lot of books in the loft, in boxes. There are also lots of pictures in frames, wrapped carefully in paper, glasses and plates, rolled-up rugs, lamps, CDs and old car seats. When we moved in, Mummy and Daddy put lots of things up there 'just until we finish decorating'. But the decorating never got finished so there are lots of things still up in the loft. Including a family of bats.

My older brother Jacob googled how to get rid of bats in your loft and it turned out bats are protected and you can't move them. So Mummy phoned the council and they sent a bat man around. William D was delighted to hear this and hung around Front Door all morning wearing his own Batman outfit waiting for the Real Bat Man to show.

William D looked a little disappointed when the Real Bat Man arrived. Especially because we couldn't open Front Door so he had to come around the back through the wet rhododendron and looked more like Aquaman when he came dripping into the kitchen. He had a big belly and not much hair on his head but as Daddy said later: 'Who knows what Batman looks like when he doesn't have his suit on?'

'He looks like Christian Bale,' Mummy said.

The bat man went up into the loft and came back a little later to tell us we had horseshoe bats. We googled them. They're light brown, with big ears and squashed up faces. Their noses do look a bit like upside-down horseshoes. Daddy said they were ugly but I thought they were amazing.

'How can we get rid of them?' Mummy asked.

'You can't,' the man said. 'They're protected.'

'I don't want to hurt them,' Mummy said. 'But can't we move them?'

The bat man shook his head. 'They're nesting at the moment, they have babies.'

Daisy and I squealed in excitement. Baby bats? This was too good to be true.

Mummy groaned. 'How did they get in?' she asked.

'There's a hole in your roof,' the bat man said.

'We'll have to block it up,' Mummy said.

'You can't,' the man said. 'The bats need to be able to come and go to bring food for the babies.'

'So we have to put up with a hole in our roof, just so the bats can get in and out?'

The bat man nodded sympathetically.

'The babies need to eat, Mummy,' Daisy said, reasonably.

'Yes,' the bat man said. 'They won't be any trouble, you'll hardly know they are there, apart from the droppings. It's probably a good idea to clean that up. You know, because you have kids, and the droppings are toxic.'

'Great,' Mummy said. 'So I need to tiptoe around them, clean up their toxic poo. Maybe I could cook for them as well? Do they eat potato waffles?'

'They only eat insects,' the bat man said. I don't think he could tell Mummy was being sarcastic.

'Perhaps we could install a revolving door for them?' Mummy said.

'A bat-flap?' Daddy suggested. Daisy and I giggled.

'That's not necessary,' the bat man said without smiling. 'They can come and go through the hole, remember?'

Mummy sighed. 'Do they need anything else?' she said. 'Blankets? Milk? The WiFi code?'

'No,' the bat man said, shaking his head. 'Just leave them alone. Once the breeding season is over they'll all go off. Then you can block up the hole.'

'Yay,' Daisy and I said.

As the bat man was leaving, he yawned and stretched,

which pulled up his jumper a little bit. William D's eyes bulged as he saw the man was wearing a utility belt. It had a torch, a penknife, a phone, some pens, and right in the middle, a big buckle with the Batman insignia on it.

The bat man finished his tea, winked at William D and walked out the back door.

Party?

Another annoying thing about Imogen is that she has her birthday just a few days after mine. Last year, to avoid clashing, I made sure to arrange my birthday celebration for the last Saturday before school finished, as she always has a massive party on the first Saturday of the holidays. That worked OK. We went wall climbing and then went to Burger Joint. This year, though, I wanted to have a big party, at home, in the garden. So I needed to make sure I organised it for the same day again, just to make sure everyone could come.

Imogen was a nightmare at school today. The first incident was when Emily and I went into the changing rooms to get our packed lunches. Emily was breathless because she was really excited that she was going to see the new *Dark Blade* film at the cinema that evening. Emily is allowed to watch all sorts of films that Mummy won't let me watch. Imogen overheard us and said she'd already seen it and smirked when I said I wasn't allowed to. I haven't even seen the last three Harry Potter films because Mummy says they're too scary. I'm extra cross about this because William D watched number six when he had a play-date over at William P's house.

Anyway, Emily popped into the loo leaving her lunchbox on the bench. Imogen came in with Hannah and Sophie and she picked up Emily's blueberry Froob yoghurt that had been sitting on the top.

'Put that back,' I said. 'That's not yours.'

'I'm just looking,' Imogen said. Then she threw it to Hannah, who threw it to Sophie, who threw it back to Imogen. I tried to grab the yoghurt in mid-air but it bounced off my fingers and through the door to the loos and landed IN A TOILET. Imogen and the others screamed with laughter and ran off just as Emily was coming back. Later on I heard that Imogen had said it was me that had done it because it had touched my fingers last. Emily heard the rumour and she was upset at first until I explained as we walked home. After lunch, in geography, Imogen kept talking about her birthday party, which I haven't been invited to. She's invited most of the class, but not Emily or me. Whenever she sees us she starts talking about it really loudly.

'We're having a band,' she said. 'And a magician, and a hog roast, and there's another food option for vegetarians and for vegans and people with nut allergies. And coeliacs.'

I don't really want to go anyway. I'd have a miserable time with Imogen bossing everyone around and making comments about how rich they are and how they're going to Barbados in the holidays. But I would like to be invited. Why can't she invite me, then I can say no politely and everything would be OK? I don't want to be friends with her, but why do we have to be enemies?

'When is your party anyway?' Emily asked her.

'The last Saturday before school breaks up,' she said.

My heart sank. 'That was when I was going to have my party,' I said. I could feel myself getting cross. My face goes white when I get cross, just like Mummy's. 'I've already told lots of people.'

'Have you sent invitations out?' she asked, smirking. She knew I hadn't.

I'm sure Imogen only decided to have it then to clash with mine. Someone must have told her. She knows she's more popular and everyone will want to go to hers instead. So now I need to decide whether to move days or just have a smaller party.

Or maybe I should cancel it altogether. What's the point of having a party if no one wants to come?

ST ANDREW'S INFANT SCHOOL

SCHOOL LUNCH REPORT

Day: Mon, Tue, Wed, Thu, Fri

Child's Name: William D

Class: Caterpillars

Today your child:
- (Hardly ate any food)
- Ate no food

Details: William D says
he is allergic to baked
beans. Could you please
phone the office
to confirm?

Signed:

Mrs Gurney

School Secretary

Bella

Today (Friday) William D came home with a School Lunch Report.

We thought it was hilarious but Mummy had to pretend she was cross with him.

'You need to eat,' she said to him. 'And you're not allergic to baked beans.'

'Sorry Mummy,' he said.

I worked on my school project after dinner. I wrote about the sitting room.

The Sitting Room

People don't sit in the sitting room very much. It's at the front of the house, just to your left as you come in through Front Door (if she's decided to open that day). There's a big bay window and you can see right up and down the street or you could if there wasn't a jungle in the front garden. There are sofas and bookshelves where we keep the sort of books that look good but people don't read. The ones we read are all stained with Ribena and scribbled on with biro and felt-tip. Some of them are so old they were scribbled on by Mummy and Daddy when they were little.

Mummy doesn't want a television in there because she wants it to be a proper, formal sitting room. And because there's no television in the sitting room, we don't go in there much. I think Mummy quite likes that no one uses it because there's at least one, mostly, tidy room in the house. Really, the only time we do go in there is when Jacob's girlfriends come around on a Friday night. Daisy, William D and I are in charge of meeting and greeting his dates and looking after them while Jacob gets ready. Usually, Jacob isn't ready and it's down to us to entertain his girlfriend (as Daddy puts it) or 'grill her' (as Mummy puts it). Mummy encourages us to ask lots of questions when Jacob's girlfriends come around, because she wants to know what sort of girl Jacob is going out with.

We all LOVE it when Jacob's girlfriends come to pick him up. When the doorbell rings we all run screaming to Front Door and try to open her. It's always better when Front Door isn't opening, though, because it means the girl has to come in through the window, or sometimes through the rhododendron. That sort of experience is a fun ice-breaker and tells you a lot about someone's character. Front Door usually plays along on these occasions. William D keeps the girl occupied by talking to her through the letterbox while Daisy runs up to tell Jacob his 'GIRLFRIEND IS HERE!' and I go to open the window in the sitting room and coax her in. Sometimes they don't want to come through the window so I run around the side and guide them through the rhododendron then help to get the spiderwebs out of their hair.

You never know what you're going to get with Jacob's girlfriends. Sometimes they're really nervous and ask questions like 'Does Jacob talk about me much?' Sometimes they seem really cross (which is not surprising when you've just had to help them pick baby spiders out of their pashmina). They often ask why Jacob couldn't pick them up instead, but I think Jacob likes his girlfriends to collect him because he's not very good at remembering where he's supposed to be and this way the girls do all the remembering for him. Also it's because he knows we like meeting all of his dates and giving them star ratings.

Jacob does not like confrontation. Mummy says he takes after Daddy. Mummy doesn't mind confrontation at all. Jacob is lovely, usually. He sometimes looks after us when Mummy and Daddy are out and he's really good at cooking mac and cheese. But he's going through an 'awkward time' as Mummy says. We don't see much of him really as he gets up late for college and sleeps a lot. Sometimes I forget all about him then suddenly he comes leaping downstairs and gives Mummy a heart attack and dives out of the front window because he's late for something. He works at an all-night garage too so he gets back at silly o'clock. He's practically nocturnal, like the bats.

As I was finishing writing about the sitting room (which turned out to have been more about Jacob than about the sitting room) the doorbell rang. It was around eight p.m. William D should really have been in bed but Mummy and Daddy always let him stay up a bit later on the weekends, especially when one of Jacob's girlfriends was coming. Otherwise he'd just be bouncing around his room with excitement and come down the stairs anyway to stare and giggle at the poor girl.

William D always gets to Front Door first. He's supposed to explain that the door is stuck and that someone is coming to help but he always forgets and says random things that he thinks will get a laugh.

'Don't panic!' he shouted through the letterbox. 'Poo head!' Then he shrieked with laughter.

I popped my head out of the sitting room window; it's a bay window so you can see the porch easily. You can climb onto the low wall at the side of the steps and over to the windowsill. We've all got the hang of it now but Mummy and Daddy are big and not very bendy so they tend to go through the rhododendron.

'Hello,' I said to the girl standing there. 'Are you Bella?'

'Yes. Hello,' the girl said. She had long brown hair with a fringe all swept across her forehead. She was wearing a lilac summer dress, which I thought Daisy might quite like.

'Don't be alarmed,' I said in a calm voice. 'The front door is stuck. You have two options. You can come in through the window, or go around the side.'

'I think I'll go around the side,' she said. She looked nervous, I thought.

'You can if you like,' I said. 'But you have to push

through a rhododendron and it's been raining so you might get your lovely dress wet.' I always try to encourage them to come in through the window.

'Oh. OK,' she said.

It took a lot of coaxing to get her up on the wall, then to make the big step over to the sill. She kept going 'Ooh! Ooh!' in a high-pitched voice.

'Is Jacob actually here?' she asked, mid-stride.

'He's upstairs getting ready,' I said. 'He always takes ages.'

Bella got in eventually, with a lot of encouragement from me. She sat on the armchair, looking around her with big frightened eyes. She was quite pretty but didn't look very mentally tough.

Daisy whispered something into William D's ear.

'Would you like a drink?' William D asked Bella.

'No thanks,' she said, still breathing heavily.

'Are you on the run?' William D asked.

'Shush, William D,' I said. 'Don't mind him. Are you at college with Jacob?'

'Yes,' she said. 'Does he . . . err, does he mention me?'

'All the time,' I said.

'No,' Daisy said.

'He does to me,' I said quickly, though it was a bit of a lie. Jacob had mentioned just today that she was coming, and what her name was, but he'd had to check on his phone as he couldn't remember if it was Bella coming tonight or someone called Charlie. Mummy had shaken her head and told him he wasn't being very respectful towards women. He'd said it wasn't his fault girls kept asking him out.

'You could say no to them,' Mummy had pointed out.

'I don't like confrontation,' he'd reminded her.

'But then they go out with you and then they text the next day,' she'd replied. 'And you have to pretend you didn't get the text or that you lost your phone, and it gets even more complicated.'

'The bit I'm trying to avoid,' Jacob had said, 'is when they are sitting in front of you and asking if you like them and you have to say no. I hate that bit. It's because I respect women that I don't want to put them through that.'

'If you respected them, you'd tell them straight,' Mummy had said.

Anyway, so there I was with Bella, trying to make conversation while we waited for Jacob, but we were interrupted by The Slug, who leaped in through the window carrying a fat, orange slug in his mouth. Bella screamed and made a fuss. Daddy had to come in and deal with things, which meant picking up The Slug and carrying him to the back of the house whilst nearly being sick.

Finally Jacob arrived, smelling of his second-favourite aftershave. He helped Bella out of the window and off they went up York Road, Bella still shaken from the slug incident.

I looked at the other two.

49

'It's a no from me, I'm afraid,' William D said. He watches too much *X-Factor*.

Daisy shrugged. 'I liked her dress.'

'What about the girl inside the dress?' I asked.

Daisy shrugged again. 'Meh.'

'Too flimsy,' I said.

'Flimsy as a coat hanger,' Daisy agreed.

Flimsy doesn't really cut it in our house.

Part Two

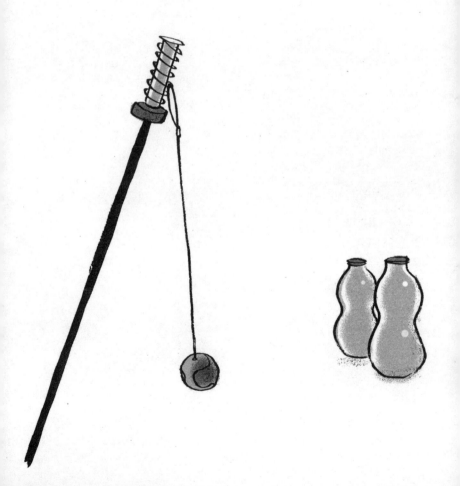

Our Street

We live on York Road, which is about fifteen minutes from our school. It's a very friendly street and we know lots of people. On Wednesday mornings, very early, the bin men come along, the truck growling, lights flashing. I sometimes wake up and listen to the men calling to each other in low voices, talking about football in the winter, or cricket in the summer. There are cars up and down the street. Mummy gets cross sometimes because she can hardly ever park outside our house.

'It's ridiculous,' Mummy said one day last summer. 'Why can't people just park in front of their own house?'

'It only takes one person to mess it up,' Daddy pointed out. 'If Mr Smith parks outside Mr Jones's house, then Mr Jones has to park outside Mr Brown's house, Mr Brown has to park outside Mr err, Pink's house, then Mr Pink . . .'

'Yes, I get it, thanks,' Mummy snapped. 'And I'm going to do something about it.'

She can be very determined when she wants to be. Daddy just shook his head.

Mummy, with help from Vicky Bellamy, Emily's

mummy, put a flyer through everyone's door and Daisy and I stapled posters to lamp-posts up and down the street.

SATURDAY 15th June there will
be a RE-PARKING day on York Rd.

Please be prepared to move your car
to a spot outside your OWN HOME.

10.00 a.m. sharp. Refreshments will be provided.

All enquiries to:

polly_deal@gmail.com (no 26)

vicky.fluffbucket@hotmail.com (no 17)

Mummy got lots of replies and everyone thought it was a brilliant idea.

'See,' Mummy said, punching Daddy on the arm. 'Mr Cynic. All people need is a little organising. Everyone wants to be a good neighbour.'

When the day came there was a sort of carnival atmosphere. Mrs Simpson made brownies and handed them out.

'I think we should wait until after everyone's moved before we bring out the refreshments,' Mummy said, 'otherwise there won't be an incentive,' but Mrs Simpson ignored her.

'Where is Mr Simpson?' Mr Coleman from next door

asked her, taking a brownie. 'I haven't seen him for ages.'

We saw Vicky Bellamy across the street, carrying a big pile of something.

'Vicky?' Mummy called. 'What are you doing? We don't need bunting, for heaven's sake.'

Vicky loves bunting. Daddy says she has bunting in her toilet. She's always trying to organise street parties. Justin from next-door-the-other-way said the tradition started with the Royal Wedding; that was before we moved here. But then there was another for the Olympics, then one when Prince George was born. She tried to arrange one for the Scottish referendum but Mr McDougall from number 6 got into a fight with Mr Campbell from number 58 at the organising committee barbecue, so it was cancelled.

The re-parking didn't work out, unfortunately. Mostly because William D took the car keys and dropped them down a drain, so we couldn't move our car. While half the street were busy trying to fish them out, Vicky Bellamy not only put the bunting up but brought tables out and put them in the middle of the road with help from Mrs Simpson, who brought more brownies and a sponge cake despite Mummy telling them to wait. So by the time we'd got our keys out no one could move their cars because of the tables.

It didn't really matter about the re-parking anyway because we all had a lovely time and got to meet loads of people in the street that we hadn't known. Mummy got a bit cross at first but eventually she just shrugged her shoulders and had a big slice of Victoria Sponge.

The day was pronounced a success, but not for the reasons Mummy had originally planned.

Two Pints Today

On Monday, I woke up when it was still dark and lay in bed worrying about my party. I knew I had to make a decision soon or it would be too late. I couldn't get back to sleep and eventually had to get up to go to the loo. The floorboards were cold under my bare feet. I raced back to my warm bed and snuggled down under the covers, sighing happily. Then I heard something outside like breaking glass. It wasn't Wednesday so it couldn't have been the recycling truck. I got up and looked out of the window and saw a milk float and a lady in a white coat on the pavement outside our house. It was Cara, who delivers our milk. She was looking down at a pattern of white spreading across the pavement, like a fallen cloud. As I watched, she shook her head and knelt down to pick up the broken glass. I'm not sure what made me go down to help her. Probably because I'm always breaking things and it's nice when someone helps you clean up afterwards. I put on my dressing gown and slippers and trotted down three flights of stairs. I grabbed a dustpan and brush from under the stairs, climbed out of the front window and jumped over to the doorstep.

Cara leaped a mile at the sound and spun around, clutching her chest.

'Sorry,' I said. 'I didn't mean to frighten you. I came to help you clean up.'

'That's OK,' she said, smiling. 'I sometimes forget there are other people in the world when I'm on my round.'

'I heard the smash,' I said. 'I've brought a dustpan and brush.'

'Thanks,' she said, smiling. She had dark skin and big teeth as white as the milk. 'I'm Cara.'

'I know,' I said. 'We met when you came around to remind my mummy she hadn't paid the bill.'

'Oh yes,' she said. 'I remember.'

We cleaned up the milk and glass together and chatted in a low whisper.

'Is it lonely, being a milk lady?' I asked.

She nodded. 'It can be. But it has its good points.'

'Free milk?' I suggested.

'Yes, that's one,' she laughed. 'And you get your day's work done nice and early so you have lots of time for other things.'

'Tell me more about being a milk lady,' I said. 'Please?'

'Shouldn't you be in bed?' she asked.

I shook my head. 'Once I'm up, I'm up,' I said.

'I suppose that was my fault for dropping the bottle and waking you,' Cara replied. She looked up and down the street. 'Look. I'm behind schedule now. I'm sorry. Thanks for helping but I'd better get back to it.'

I must have looked very disappointed, because she put her head to one side. 'Tell you what,' she said. 'I have to go right down to the end of York Road and then back again. If you like, you can ride on the float with me up and back. I can tell you all about the job.'

'Yes please,' I said.

York Road is a cul-de-sac. Right down the far end is a row of bollards blocking a path that leads to the little park where we play sometimes. They cut the grass there, so you can run without getting tangled in nettles and long, wet grass. Anyway, that's how I came to be riding on a milk float at 4.36 a.m. on a wet Monday. Cara did most of the talking. She was very funny and it turned out she'd been delivering milk for a long time.

'One of the best things about the job is that it has Transferable Skills,' she said. 'You can deliver milk anywhere. Except China.'

'Why not China?' I asked. 'Don't they have milk floats?'

'No milk floats. No milk,' she said. 'They're lactose-intolerant.'

Cara also knew a lot about the people on York Road. She told me Mrs Simpson was on her third husband and no one was quite sure what had happened to the first two but there were *suspicions*. Mrs Simpson liked full cream milk. Then Cara told me Shouty Dad from across the road had a stressful job in the City and the Dukes went through twelve bottles of orange juice every week.

'Twelve!' she said. 'Are they bathing in it, do you think?'

I helped carry bottles of milk and orange juice and yoghurt cartons to the doorways. Cara said I was a great help and she didn't get cross even when I tripped over a cat and dropped a box of eggs.

'No use crying over spilt milk,' Cara said. 'Or smashed eggs. Did you know I used to deliver milk to the Northern Territory of Australia? All the way from Queensland on the East Coast. The longest milk-run in the world.'

'Wow,' I said.

Cara dropped me back at our house just before five a.m.

'Thanks for helping me, Chloe,' she said.

'Can I do it again sometime?' I asked.

Cara frowned. 'I don't think your parents would thank me for getting you up so early every day.'

'What if I'm already awake and can't sleep?'

She laughed again. 'I'm going to try very hard not to wake you up again, but if you do happen to be lying awake one morning, and you hear me, then yes. You can come for a ride, but I want you to tell your parents, promise?'

'I promise,' I said.

'Bye, Chloe.'

'Bye, Cara.'

The Bats

On Saturday, I was woken early by Shouty Dad across the street. I didn't mind because I enjoy watching him get cross. It was a little nippy so I dragged my duvet across to the window seat. My breath frosted the glass.

I often like to take a book and sit on the window seat. I'd brought up some cushions from the sitting room to make it more comfortable there. I don't read much when I'm on that seat, I just stare out of the window watching people. Watching people is pretty much my favourite thing to do. I can see three houses on the opposite side of the street. The Mellors' house on the left, the Bellamys' house on the right, where Emily lives, and the Dukes' house directly opposite us. In the daytime I like to watch them all come and go. The Dukes especially, because of Shouty Dad. The Dukes have three children who are all quite little and they are completely mad: the little boy runs off all the time, even more than William D, and the girls argue and fight and play practical jokes on Shouty Dad to wind him up and make him shout even louder. The mummy doesn't do much except make a big fuss of them when they fall over and she gives them endless sweets, whether they've been good or bad.

The daddy just shouts ALL THE TIME. That's why he's called Shouty Dad. Mummy told me everyone in the town calls him that. I quite like it when he gets really cross and goes red and even from across the street I can see the veins stand out on his forehead.

Clematis came in and mewed at me before jumping up beside me to see what I was looking at. I scratched his ears as I watched Shouty Dad trying to pack his car. It was all full up like they were going on holiday somewhere. Shouty Dad was having trouble opening the boot and was shouting at Mrs Duke, who I think was still in the house.

'WHY HAVE WE GOT SO MUCH STUFF?' he yelled. 'WE'RE ONLY GOING FOR THE WEEKEND!'

Daisy padded into my room looking sleepy and crawled under the duvet with me. She loves watching Shouty Dad as much as I do. The smell of bacon frying drifted up the stairs and my tummy growled.

By pushing really hard and slamming the boot closed quickly, Mr Duke managed to get everything in. But then Mrs Duke came out of the house with a huge soft bag.

'WHAT'S THAT?' he yelled, pointing. His voice went all high-pitched when he said 'THAT'. Daisy giggled.

Mrs Duke said something I couldn't hear and Shouty Dad went into proper meltdown. He slumped to the ground and looked like he might be crying. Daisy giggled. After that it was time to get his children into the car.

Two of them got in but the little one had disappeared and when Shouty Dad went off to look for him, the other two got out and opened the boot, unzipped a bag and started looking for something. It sounds a bit mean to say but I'm glad Mummy and Daddy aren't friends with the Dukes. They're always squabbling. Sometimes it's better to observe from a distance. Like when they film nature documentaries.

Shouty Dad came out of the house with the smallest child under his arm and managed to lock the front door with difficulty. Mrs Duke was in the car already and called something to him through the window.

'I KNOW!' he yelled back. 'WHAT DO YOU THINK I'M DOING?'

Then he saw what the older children were up to in the boot. At that point he really flipped. He said some words that I'm not allowed to write down and Daisy didn't know what they meant. Eventually they got everything and everyone into the car and drove off. I heard one last shout from Shouty Dad as they drove past our house.

'THAT'S WHY I BOUGHT THE SAT-NAV!' he screamed.

It went quiet after that and I was about to say to Daisy that we should go down to breakfast when we heard a squeaking sound from above.

'Is that the bats?' she asked.

'Yes,' I said. 'I sometimes hear them at night. I think

the mummy and daddy bat go out and get food for them. When they come back the little babies go bonkers.'

'Oh sweeeeeet!' she said.

'I know,' I said.

'What sort of food do they bring?' she asked.

'Insects, I think. Moths and beetles.'

Daisy scrunched up her face. 'That doesn't sound very nice.'

'No,' I said.

'Why don't we take them some yummy food?' Daisy said.

I frowned. 'I don't think we're supposed to do that.'

'Why not?' Daisy asked. I like that Daisy thinks I know everything, and I try not to disappoint her by saying I don't know.

'I just have a feeling Mummy wouldn't like it,' I said.

'Has she told you we can't?'

'No,' I admitted.

'If we fed them, and she found out, and got cross, we could just say we didn't know we weren't supposed to,' Daisy said. My sister is quite logical sometimes.

'OK,' I said, grinning. 'Let's do it, straight after breakfast.'

William D came into the room, just in time to hear Daisy say, 'We can feed a bacon sandwich to the bats!'

'YES!' William D shouted, punching the air. 'Butties for the batties!'

'You're not coming,' I said straight away.

But then his lip wobbled. 'Mummy!' he cried.

'OK, OK,' I said, hurriedly. 'You can come, but only if you don't tell Mummy about this, Family Deal?'

'Family Deal,' he said.

At breakfast Daisy and I wrapped up a whole bacon sandwich in a napkin to give to the bats. One by one we left the table so as to not arouse suspicion. Once we'd assembled in my room I unwrapped the bacon sandwich.

'They're going to love it,' Daisy said.

'Better than yucky bugs,' William D agreed.

'Let's do this,' I said in a firm voice. Then William D ran off.

'Where are you going?' I asked.

'To get changed,' William D shouted as he raced down the stairs.

'You don't need to get changed,' I said, exasperated. 'Daisy why did you have to go and tell him about feeding the bats?'

'Sorry,' she said. 'You know what? I think I might get changed too.'

'Why?'

'I don't want to get my top dirty,' she said.

I sighed. I had a bad feeling about this.

I really don't understand why Daisy cares so much about how she looks. That day she was wearing a pair of denim shorts over white leggings, a spotty navy top and her favourite rose hairclip. She had her hair in a side parting with a ponytail to one side. It was true she looked very neat and tidy, and I suppose pretty too, but was it really worth all that effort? Daisy and I are very different in lots of ways.

I was wearing my black saggy leggings with the hole in the knee and my old blue T-shirt with the frayed hem that Daddy had brought back from one of the companies he once did some work for. It had the words Bri-Tech on the back because that was the name of the company. I liked it because it was comfortable and I never had to worry about getting it muddy or torn. Mummy sometimes tried to get me to wear nice clothes and gave me lectures about taking pride in my appearance but I never really feel comfortable in skirts and I hate brushing my hair.

Daisy came back wearing similar clothes to the ones she'd had on before.

'You're wearing another nice top,' I said.

'This old thing?' she asked, looking pleased.

I sighed again. 'Are you ready?'

'Ready as a suitcase,' she said.

Ever since Daisy and her friend Tamsin learned about similes in Year Two, they use them all the time and just make them up randomly. So in the morning Daisy might say 'I'm as hungry as a lorry.' Or at bedtime she'll be 'as tired as a hat stand.'

William D was wearing his Batman suit, of course.

He was carrying a bag stuffed full of 'useful things'. He kept peering about and bumping into things because the visibility from inside the mask isn't great.

The stairs to the loft are hidden behind a little door that grown-ups have to duck to go through. We crept up carefully, not wanting to disturb the bats, who would be sleeping because they're nocturnal. Our plan was to leave the bacon sandwich in a dish on the floor under the sleeping bats, so when they woke up they'd have a tasty breakfast snack.

I'd wanted to get a plastic bowl or something from the kitchen but Mummy had been in there all morning, singing songs from *Frozen* over and over again then getting cross at herself for having the songs from *Frozen* stuck in her head. So I'd had to take the plate from the sitting room which had William D's footprints on it in glaze from when he was a baby. I would put it back after the bats had eaten the bacon sandwich, before anyone noticed.

The plan went perfectly at first. I shuffled forward in the gloom. The only light was from the bare bulb on the staircase outside. I could just about see the tiny little bats all huddled together in a corner. I put the plate down and started backing away, trying not to disturb the little creatures as they shivered and muttered to one another. The bat man had said that if we absolutely HAD to go into the loft we mustn't shine lights on them or make any noise.

So what did William D do? He shone his torch right at them and shouted: 'Commissioner Gordon calling Batman, Commissioner Gordon calling Batman!'

Immediately the bats went bananas and the loft was filled with the fluttering of wings as a thousand million black shapes started whizzing around us. I could feel the wind from their wings. I tried not to scream. I tried to hold my breath. I tried to stay still. But then William D dropped his torch and it went out, plunging us into darkness. He let out a blood-curdling screech and ran for the door. I couldn't control myself any more. I panicked and raced after him. And as I ran, ONE OF THE BATS TOUCHED MY CHEEK!

I didn't think they were so cute after that, I can tell you. William D was screaming, Daisy was screaming, I was screaming. The bats were probably screaming too, though so high we couldn't hear them. We raced downstairs, tumbling down the stairs and landing together in a heap at the bottom, shaking with fright. I had toxic bat poo on my shoe. Daisy was as white as a sheet. William D ran into his room and hid under the bed. Mummy came leaping up the stairs thinking we were being murdered.

When she found out what we'd really been up to I think she thought about murdering us herself. Especially when she discovered that William D's plate had got smashed into a dozen pieces. I must have stood on it in the confusion.

We all decided it was best if we stayed out of Mummy's hair for the rest of the morning so I came up to my room to work on my Project. I wrote loads about William D's room. I hadn't meant to write so much but there are so many stories to tell, especially about William D.

William D's Room

William D's room is on the first floor. Next to Mummy and Daddy's room. If you look at the toys and posters in his room you can tell he really likes Batman, Superman, Spider-Man, Aquaman and My Little Pony. Mummy says having two older sisters is a good influence on him. There's not much more to say about William D's room except it's always in chaos, except for five minutes every day just after Mummy's tidied it but before William D has started hurling his toys around again. But really the most interesting thing about William D's room is William D.

There are four Williams in Caterpillar Class at the infant school. William P, William H, Little William and William D. Everyone calls our William William D. Otherwise how would they know which William they were talking about? His teachers call him William D, the other mummies call him William D, Gabi who teaches the little ones to swim at the leisure centre calls him William D. They all call him William D in Sainsbury's too. They know him well in there. Ever since we moved to Weyford we've gone to that Sainsbury's two or three times a week and every time he goes in William D runs off from Mummy and hits a big shiny red button near the Customer Service desk. Every time. This sets off a piercing alarm and makes the lights flicker until someone has to come and reset it.

'I really don't know why they put that alarm at a height a four-year-old can reach,' Mummy says, tutting. 'And why make it red? Of course he wants to press it.'

She's not the only one who tuts. Mummy gets looks. Why is it that grown-ups don't notice when other grown-ups are giving them looks? Or maybe it's just Mummy. The manager of Sainsbury's is always very nice about the alarm thing but I can tell that he's wondering why Mummy can't stop her child from setting off the alarm EVERY time he comes into the shop.

Anyway, everyone else knows him as William D. I suppose the name just stuck, so we call him William D now, too.

ST ANDREW'S INFANT SCHOOL

INCIDENT/ACCIDENT REPORT

Day: Mon, Tue, Wed, Thu, Fri

Child's Name: William D

Class: Caterpillars

Details of Incident/Accident:

William D was hit
on the head by a
musical instrument.
He seems ok.

Signed: Mrs Gurney

School Secretary

William D Extras

There were some things I wrote in my report about William D that I decided I couldn't really hand in to Mrs Fuller, even though one of them had some really good dialogue. Doing all the speech marks takes AGES so I was really annoyed and didn't want to have to write it all again. So I cut them out and pasted the remaining bits on a fresh sheet.

I think I was right to take this bit out though:

William D talks about poo a lot, which he definitely didn't learn from me. When Mummy was trying to get him to do his poos in the potty, she told him once that one of them looked like a dinosaur. So somehow we ended up rating his poos by saying what dinosaur they looked like. You know, to encourage him? So a little one might be a raptor, a really long one might be a brontosaurus, a pointy one might be a triceratops. Once he called out to say he'd done a woolly mammoth.

'That's not a dinosaur,' Mummy said, going to look. 'Mammoths are hairy.'

'This hairy too,' William D pointed out, showing Mummy the contents of the potty.

Mummy was quiet for a bit.

'What on earth have you been eating, William D?' she asked.

There's lots more I could write about William D. Like how he usually comes out of school with a note reporting something that happened that day. There are two types of notes: School Lunch Reports and Incident/Accident Reports.

Yesterday he brought back an Accident Report.

Mummy asked William D about this as we were walking home from school and he said, 'I accidentally didn't wait for my turn on the instrument.'

'What do you mean you "accidentally didn't wait"?' Mummy asked.

'Well,' he said. 'I said I'd wait for Sophie to finish and then I waited for a bit and then I suddenly stopped waiting. Accidentally.'

'You tried to grab it from her?'

'Yes.'

'You shouldn't grab, William D,' Mummy said. 'No wonder you were hurt.' Then she asked: 'What sort of instrument was it, anyway?'

'A sharp one,' William D replied, rubbing his ear.

'I hope you've learned your lesson,' Mummy said.

'Sorry, Mummy,' William D said. William D is very good at saying sorry. He's had a lot of practice, Mummy says.

BOOMball

The first summer we lived here Daisy and I got a Swingball set to play with in the new garden. We went mad for it at first but when school started and the weather wasn't so good, we stopped playing it. Then one Sunday last autumn it was scorching hot and we wanted to play again but we couldn't because the rackets were lost in the long grass and the string holding the ball to the pole had got wet and snapped. So Daddy took us to Home 'n Garden Megastore to buy some string because he was going anyway because he ALWAYS goes to Home 'n Garden Megastore at the weekend. We got some more paint testing pots and William D got a Spider-Man DVD, which I think he already had but it doesn't really matter because he doesn't mind watching things over and over. And Daddy grabbed a ball of string but when we got home we realised he'd bought elasticated string instead of normal string.

'Never mind,' Daddy said. 'Let's try it with this.'

So he attached the elasticated string to the ball and the pole and then we realised we didn't have the rackets any more so William D ran into the playroom and came back with the only bat he could find, which was one of those ones with a drum skin on it that goes BOOM! when you hit the ball.

'It's no good with only one racket,' I said doubtfully, but Daddy just tutted and told me to use my imagination.

So BOOMball was invented. One person (The Chucker) throws the ball up in the air and ducks while the person with the racket (The Boomer) smashes the ball as hard as possible, trying to make the biggest BOOM! The ball flies off into space, then the elasticated string stretches tight and snaps the ball back towards everyone (The Duckers) and you have to avoid being hit. William D gets hit a lot and cries every time but you can't stop him playing because then he cries even more. The only other rule is that if Mummy comes out you have to whistle and pretend you're just playing a normal game of Swingball.

'Why does William D have his bike helmet on?' she might ask.

'We're going to fire him out of a cannon,' Daddy says and we all laugh, even Mummy, though sometimes she looks as if she suspects Daddy might very well fire William D out of a cannon one day if left to his own devices too long. One of the good things about BOOMball is the ball is attached to the pole. Attaching the ball to the pole is very important because if William D sees a ball that's not attached to something, then he'll grab it and run off. He can't help himself. Daddy once said that it was because William D was born during the Rugby World Cup Final and the need to pick up balls and run with them is imprinted in him. He's really fast too and very strong. You have to tackle him to catch him. Then one of you has to hold him down while the others prise the ball from his fingers. He does not give up easily, I can tell you. If he gets away he'll stash the ball somewhere then forget where it is. Sometimes we find little collections of balls of various sizes stuck under a bush.

He once tried to run off with the BOOMball ball but the elastic string went tight and snapped the ball clean out of his fingers and it went smack into his face. So he seems to have learned his lesson.

Over the months we've added new and better rules to BOOMball. If Daddy is one of The Duckers he is no longer allowed to pick one of us up to 'use as a shield'. If you manage to hit the returning ball a second time you get double points and if you catch the ball you get a point and you get to be The Boomer. Anyway, today we went out after lunch to play. But Mummy caught us before we got far and put us on slug patrol instead.

The only area outside which is well tended is the 'kitchen garden', close to the kitchen door. This was already there when we moved in and it's well tended because this is the bit Mummy looks after. She grows herbs there: parsley, mint, tarragon, rosemary and basil. I know all their names because Mummy often sends me or Daisy out to collect some while she's making dinner.

She also grows courgettes, onions, sweetcorn and tomatoes. I like going out to get herbs, but I don't like my other job in the kitchen garden, which is getting rid of the snails and slugs.

Today I knelt down and stared for ages at a little snail sitting on a tomato leaf, chomping away. She (it looked like a she) was all slimy, except for the shell, which was caked with something dark. She'd left a little shiny, silvery trail behind her across the leaf and I decided her name was Sylvia. Eventually I steeled myself, held my breath and grabbed the shell firmly. Daisy made gagging noises next to me and William D shrieked in excitement. Sylvia didn't want to come away from the plant and I had to pull quite hard. But she came off eventually and I dropped her into the flowerpot Mummy had given me. After that it was a bit easier. I got six snails and four slugs. One of the slugs was orange, the others black. I used a bit of wood to pick up the slugs because they were just so disgusting.

I took them into the kitchen.

'What should I do with them now, Mummy?' I asked.

'Don't bring them in here!' she said. 'Take them into the garden and squash them under your foot.'

I stared at her in horror. 'You want me to kill them? Even Sylvia?'

'Well, what else are you going to do with snails and slugs?'

'Feed them to the cat?' Daisy suggested.

'Can't we just throw them into the bushes?' I asked.

'No, they'll come back,' Mummy said. 'You can take them down the road to the park if you like. They won't come back from there.'

It was raining a bit and I didn't really feel like going all the way down to the park, and that's when I had the clever idea of throwing them over the fence into Mr Coleman's garden. Mr Coleman has vegetables, so Sylvia and her friends might decide it was less fuss just to stay there. About thirty seconds after I'd thrown the snails over the fence there was a knock on Front Door.

William D got there first and shouted through the letterbox. 'The door's stuck, go away!'

'You haven't even tried it yet,' Mummy said, pulling on Front Door, which suddenly decided to open. (I think Front Door senses when there's going to be some fun and opens up to kick things off.) A man with a bald head was standing on the mat carrying a little plastic bag. It was Mr Coleman. I knew immediately what was in the bag.

'I think these are yours,' Mr Coleman said, holding out the bag to Mummy. Mummy took the bag and looked inside.

'I don't remember ordering any snails,' Mummy said. 'Perhaps it was my husband?'

Mr Coleman didn't laugh, in fact he looked grumpier than ever. 'They came from your garden,' Mr Coleman said.

'I really don't think so,' Mummy said.

'That's Sylvia,' William D said, peering into the bag and giving the game away.

Daisy gave him a furious look.

'They were thrown over the fence,' Mr Coleman said. 'One landed on my head.'

We all looked at his head. Now he mentioned it, there did seem to be a sticky, shiny spot right on top of the baldest bit.

'As if it wasn't enough your feral children whooping and shrieking at all hours, and playing some very noisy ball games, now I have to put up with having gastropods hurled at me.'

'I'm very sorry about this,' Mummy said. 'I think I know who might be responsible.'

As she said it she gave me a bit of a fierce look but I could tell she wasn't very angry. I think she was trying not to laugh. 'I'm the only person allowed to say mean things about my children,' she sometimes says.

'Well, thanks for returning these,' Mummy said, starting to close Front Door.

'Just one more thing,' Mr Coleman said. 'While I'm here.'

'Yes?' Mummy said, patiently.

'Are you going to do anything about the weeds in your back garden? I spend hours every week digging out dandelions and buttercups, but the first puff of wind blows thousands more spores over the fence from your side.'

'The garden is my husband's domain,' Mummy said gravely. 'I shall pass your request on to him.'

'Thank you,' Mr Coleman said, then he turned and stomped off down the steps.

Once he'd gone, Mummy gave us A Look, and handed us the bag of gastropods. 'Get rid of them,' she said. 'Properly this time, make sure they don't come back.'

Daisy and I took them down to the park and let them go. All except Sylvia, who we'd grown quite attached to. I took her home and put her in the empty water glass next to my bed to keep her safe until I thought of what to do with her. I put a coaster on top of the glass to stop her escaping and dropped in a couple of tomato leaves so she'd have something to eat.

'Why is Sylvia more special than the others?' Daisy asked, tapping the glass.

'Once you've given something a name,' I explained, 'it's under your protection.'

ST ANDREW'S INFANT SCHOOL

INCIDENT/ACCIDENT REPORT

Day: Mon, Tue, Wed, Thu, Fri

Child's Name: William D

Class: Caterpillars

Details of Incident/Accident:

William D was
bitten by a farm
animal. The skin
was not broken.

Signed:

Mrs Gurney

School Secretary

Steamers

Today was Monday and I showed some of my project to Mrs Fuller, just the bits about my room and William D's room. I was a bit nervous. I'd put lots of work into it so far and I was a bit worried she might say it wasn't what she was looking for at all.

'It's just the first draft,' I mumbled as she quickly read through the piece about my room.

'This must have taken hours to do, Chloe,' she said. 'I think this is brilliant, and I can't wait to read the rest.'

'I like writing about my house,' I told her. It was true, I hadn't been sure about this project at first because the house is a bit of a mess, but the more I wrote, the more I could see the good things about it and how the not-so-good bits aren't as important.

'It's not just the house though, Chloe,' Mrs Fuller said. 'Look again at the section you wrote about William D's room. It's not really about his room so much, but about him.'

And she's right. The more I write about the house, the more I realise I can't write about the rooms and the garden and the street without writing about the people who live in them, and the more I realise how special they all are. I decided to write some more as soon as I got home. I was starting to get excited about the My House project.

As we were walking up York Road after school William D tugged my sleeve and whispered 'That man is steaming.'

I looked to where he was pointing and saw Shouty Dad on the pavement outside his house. He was just standing there SMOKING A CIGARETTE! William D doesn't know what cigarettes are and calls them 'steamers'. I didn't know Mr Duke smoked. I don't know anyone who smokes apart from Mr Campbell at number 58 who throws his cigarette butts out of the first floor window into the front garden.

Mr Duke looked really sad and cross. Then someone must have called to him from inside his house because he turned around and screamed: 'I'LL BE IN IN A MINUTE!'

Shouty Dad is always shouty. But there was something different about the way he shouted today. And the look on his face as he sucked on his 'steamer' one more time before dropping it in the gutter made me feel a bit worried for him. I hope he's OK.

I got home and went straight up to my room to work on my project, only to find disaster had struck.

The glass was empty; Sylvia had gone missing.

I tried to follow the snail trail but it faded out after a bit. Sylvia was loose somewhere in our house.

'What on earth were you up to today?' Mummy said, reading William D's Accident Report when we got home. 'I thought you went on an excursion to look at the castle?'

'We did, but there were some animals in the field next to the castle,' William D said.

'What sort of animals?'

'They had horns,' William D said.

'What, goats? Reindeer?' Mummy said. 'Okapi?'

'I don't know,' William D replied.

'And why weren't any of the teachers able to identify these exotic animals?' Mummy said. 'What do they learn at teacher training college these days? The problem with these notes is they raise more questions than they answer.'

Decision Time

On Tuesday I woke in a panic. I still hadn't done anything about the party and I was starting to worry about it. I asked Mummy at breakfast and she said it would be OK to have it at our house but that I needed to get on with things because people would get booked up. I talked to Emily about it at lunchtime.

'The problem is,' I said, 'if I have it on the first Saturday of the holidays then I bet a lot of people won't be able to come anyway.'

'Have you tried asking?' Emily said.

'I asked Hannah, and she said she was going camping as soon as school broke up.'

'Well, what about the Sunday of the weekend before?'

'Sunday?' I hadn't really considered that. It was only one day after Imogen's party, which wasn't ideal, as everyone would make comparisons, but it was worth thinking about. I bit my lip, mulling it over.

Emily rolled her eyes, impatiently. She doesn't worry about things as much as I do. 'Just pick a day, tell your mummy that's when you want the party and get her to send out invitations. Loads of people will come.'

But I'm not sure. What if they don't? And also I'm worried that if I did have a party at our house it would be a disaster. Front Door wouldn't open, and it would rain and the rhododendron would soak everyone, and the garden would be a mess, and people would laugh at the Megadeath mural and the flappy wallpaper. I decided I would talk to Mummy that night and make a final decision.

But when Mummy collected us from Emily's house she was in a real grump. She'd had a bad day at work. She'd been let down by her boss Declan again.

'He's the boss, and he takes more sick days than the rest of the company put together,' she said when we got home.

'Tell me about it,' Daddy said. 'Nick took the morning off to go to the dentist.' As usual he wasn't letting Mummy have her moan.

'Hmm,' Mummy said, crossly. Her earlobes went white, which is a sign she's cross.

'He's having yet another crown fitted,' Daddy said. 'His jaw has more crowns than the Tower of London.'

Mummy didn't say anything.

'Did you hear my joke?' Daddy asked.

'Yes,' Mummy said. Her cheeks had gone a little red. That's another sign.

Daddy had been working from home today and I think Mummy doesn't really believe he does very much actual work when he's at home and could spend more time helping her with the school run or slashing rhododendrons.

When Mummy says Daddy is working from home she does little speech marks with her fingers when she says the word 'working'.

I think this is sarcasm.

I can tell she's at her wit's end with us all.

Anyway, so I didn't talk to her about the party that night. In particular I didn't want to ask about the garden being tidied because Mummy would have got even crosser with Daddy for not doing his jobs.

SCHOOL LUNCH REPORT

Day: Mon, Tue, Wed, Thu, Fri

Child's Name: William D

Class: Caterpillars

Today your child:

- Hardly ate any food
- Ate no food

Details: He scraped it off his plate into William P's Skylanders bag. Pls call the office.

Signed:

Mrs Gurney

School Secretary

Family Deal

I didn't talk to Mummy about the party on Wednesday night either. Mummy called us all into the kitchen after bathtime. It was a full family meeting, apart from Jacob because nobody knew where he was.

'Now, everybody,' she said. 'I think there needs to be a few changes around here. A Family Deal.'

A Family Deal is when we all promise to do something. Family because the whole family has to do it. Deal because that's who we are: The Deals.

Mummy went on. 'Today was a very difficult day for a number of reasons.'

'Like what?' Daisy asked.

'Well,' Mummy said, 'I was late for work this morning because of Front Door. Whilst dropping you off, Ellen Downing thought it necessary to point out there was a ladder in my tights and my shoes looked 'good value'. She didn't bother to point out I had a caterpillar on my cardigan making a cocoon. My colleagues left it until lunchtime to point that out.'

Mummy was counting off things on her fingers. She'd got to four but I thought it was only three.

'Also, no one did the washing-up this morning,' she continued. 'No one made their beds and no one emptied the cats' litter tray. These are all jobs you children agreed to do in exchange for pocket money.'

We all sat with our eyes down. Quietly. I felt bad about not doing my jobs. I don't really know why I didn't do them. I suppose I just don't really think about things like that, and there's always something else going on in our house, like BOOMball or bat feeding.

'And you, William D,' Mummy went on. 'Look at your star chart.'

He has a lot of star charts, William D. It's to encourage him to do things, or discourage him from doing other things. The one at the moment is to try to stop him coming home from school with notes like the one he got today about putting his dinner in William P's Skylanders bag.

'But what if I fall over and bump my head?' he asked. 'What if Oscar pushes me into the girls' toilets and I slip over again?'

'I'm not talking about Accident Reports so much,' Mummy said. 'I mean the reports about you not eating your lunch.'

So every day when he doesn't bring home a note he gets a star, unless he's done something really naughty. When the star chart is full he gets a Pokémon toy. Daisy and I are wondering whether we could get star charts too. We always eat our lunch. Anyway, today William D's star chart was empty.

'It has a black hole,' he said. 'It sucks all the stars in.'
But the truth was he hadn't got any because every day
he did at least one naughty thing.

'We're a little disappointed,' Daddy said.

Mummy gave him a look. 'And as for you,' she said
to him, 'what about *your* jobs?'

Daddy blinked in surprise.

'I'm working from home,' he said.

'You didn't have a lunch break? No time for one or
two little jobs? You're in charge of outside,' she said,
pointing out of the window. 'The bins weren't taken
out this week. The wobbly gate still hasn't been mended
and you haven't even made a start on mowing the lawn.'

'I can't find the mower,' Daddy reminded her.

William D wagged a finger at Daddy and said, 'We
all need to pull our weight.' Which made Daisy and me
giggle until Mummy glared at us.

'I need a break,' she said.

'Look,' Daddy said. 'Why don't you go up to London
this weekend, you've been saying you want to see your
sister? Stay the night, relax. While you're away we'll
straighten the house out.'

Mummy looked at him with narrow eyes. 'If I'm not
here to micro-manage, then nothing will get done.'

'When I was a boy,' Daddy said. 'My father took me
to the swimming pool to teach me to swim. Hated the
idea of putting my head under the water, though, and
refused to get in. So do you know what he did?'

'No. What?' Daisy asked, wide-eyed.

'He threw me in at the deep end,' Daddy said. 'That was the only way. Sink or swim, you see?'

We were all quiet for a moment, then I spoke.

'He threw you in the deep end?'

'Yep.'

'Even though you couldn't swim?'

'That's right.'

'Grandpa Jim's really mean,' Daisy said.

'Did you drown?' William D asked.

Later, when we were watching television, Mummy came in.

'OK, it's decided,' she said. 'I'm going to London tomorrow morning and I won't be back until Sunday teatime. While I'm away, I want you all to clean this house top-to-toe, back-to-front and up-and-down. And I want the lawn mowed and the rhododendron cut back. OK?'

'OK,' said Daddy.

'Yes, Mummy,' Daisy and I said.

'Mission accepted, Roger,' William D said. We've tried to explain to him that when people in films say 'Roger' they mean 'I understand'. But he thinks there's someone called Roger who everyone's talking to.

'You girls have loads of old toys in your rooms that you never play with,' Mummy went on. 'I'd like you to put the unwanted things into a bin-liner and we can donate it to the school so they can sell it all at the Summer Fair.'

We nodded.

'Oh, and John,' Mummy said to Daddy. 'I know it's not your area of expertise, working in IT and everything, but could you please look at the computer? It's running very slowly.'

'OK,' he said again, nodding quickly. He must have known he was really in trouble because normally he'll do anything to get out of fixing the computer.

Chip Shop Charlie

When the doorbell rang on Friday evening, we all knew what it meant. It was time for Jacob's date with a new girl called Charlie. We knew she was coming because Jacob had been quite excited about it for once and had given us all an instruction to be on our best behaviour. Front Door hadn't opened for ages so I hardly ever tried to open her. William D, who'd been excited about this all day, got to the door first and opened the letterbox.

'Stay calm!' he shouted.

'Let me talk to her,' I said, gently pushing him aside. 'Hello, are you Charlie?' I called as Daisy thundered past and ran up the stairs, hiccupping with excitement.

'Err . . . yes. Is Jacob here?'

'Yes, but he's not ready, would you like to come in and wait?'

'Yes please . . . Can you open the door?'

'No. It's stuck.'

'Oh.'

'CALM DOWN!' William D bellowed.

'Shush! She *is* calm,' I said.

I called through to Charlie, setting out the available options for getting into the house.

'So what's it to be?' I asked. 'Window, or rhododendron?'

'Gosh, it's like a Choose Your Own Adventure,' she said.

Charlie sensibly chose to come in through the window. The girls that come in through the window tend to last longer. Daisy came rushing in to watch Charlie's technique. She managed to get in without showing her knickers, which is tricky.

She stood and smiled at us. We smiled back.

William D waved an arm around, showing off the room.

'Behold!' he said, before bowing.

'What a lovely room,' Charlie said, giving a curtsey in return. We giggled.

We sat her down on the armchair and William D asked her if she wanted a drink.

'Yes please, just some water?'

'Coming right up,' William D said and charged off to the kitchen. Very polite, I thought, giving Charlie a mental *tick*. Daisy made a note in her little book.

We sat down on the sofa opposite and smiled at her. She was quite pretty, with long dark hair. She wore a little jacket over a bright orange top and a skirt. I thought she had a lot of make-up on but I could tell Daisy was smitten. Charlie looked familiar, like I'd seen her before, though I was sure she'd never been on a date with Jacob.

'Err, will Jacob be long?' Charlie asked after we'd smiled at her for a bit.

'Probably,' I said. I knew I'd have to do all the talking as Daisy tends to just stare with her mouth open. 'He sometimes forgets when he has dates.'

'Does he have a lot of dates, then?' Charlie asked. She was smiling a little.

'Oops!' I said as Daisy punched my arm. 'Not a lot of dates, no.'

'One or two a week, at the most,' Daisy said.

Charlie raised her eyebrows. 'And does he ever see the same girl more than once?'

'Oh yes.'

'Well, that's good to know,' Charlie said.

'Oh hang on, you said the SAME girl?' Daisy suddenly said. 'No. He sometimes sees more than one girl at the same time. That's what I thought you meant.'

Now it was my turn to punch Daisy on the arm. I gave her a glare for good measure.

William D came back in, without any water but carrying Buzz Lightyear. He hopped up onto the sofa between me and Daisy.

'Do you have a job?' I asked. Daisy pulled out her notebook, waiting for the answer.

'I have a part-time job at the chip shop,' Charlie said.

'THAT'S where I've seen you before,' I said, clapping a hand to my forehead.

'Oh yes,' Charlie replied. 'Everyone's seen me in the

chip shop, wearing my yellow T-shirt and my hygienic hat. Chip Shop Charlie, they call me. However hard I try, I can't get the smell of vinegar out of my hair. But I'm also a full-time student at the college.'

'Is that where you met Jacob?' I asked.

'No, actually,' she said. 'I met him in the pharmacy. I was buying something to try to mask the vinegar smell. He was buying some deoderising fungal foot powder.'

'Oh yes, he has terribly smelly feet,' I said.

'He said it was for his father,' Charlie said, smiling again.

'Slow down, slow down,' Daisy said. She writes very slowly. I keep telling her that drawing animal faces in each 'o' and love hearts over each 'i' slows her down too much.

'Do you like college?' I asked. But Charlie was saved from having to answer by the arrival of Jacob. I think he must have remembered Charlie was coming because he usually took much longer than this to get ready. He was wearing his favourite shirt as well and I wondered if he'd put on extra foot powder.

'Hi,' he said.

'Hi,' Charlie replied.

'You ready?'

'I am,' she said, standing up.

'You look great,' Jacob said.

'Thanks,' Charlie said.

'Have this lot been annoying you?' he asked, pointing

to us where we sat watching their conversation with interest, though it hadn't been very exciting so far, I had to admit.

'Not at all,' she said. 'They've been very sweet. You have a lovely family.'

'S'pose,' Jacob said, looking at us. Then he winked. Jacob went to Front Door and opened her with a flourish.

Charlie blinked in surprise. 'I thought you said it was stuck,' she said to me.

'Jacob has a way of making things happen,' I said.

'We'll see,' Charlie said as she walked out.

'It's a big yes from me,' William D said once she'd gone.

'And me,' Daisy added.

'That makes three of us,' I said.

Lost Weekend

We waved Mummy off the next morning. Daddy even held back the rhododendron so she could get her suitcase through. I felt sad when she drove off. I had this silly thought that she wouldn't come back. It was just the four of us because Jacob hadn't got home till very late and Daddy said to let him sleep. It was a nice sunny day and we ate breakfast outside on the rusty iron table that had been here already when we moved in. I could hear mowers droning and groaning up and down the street. In our garden we could hear bees and crickets. As I finished my Shreddies, a little ant crawled out of the weeds and over my bare foot, tickling me.

'Right,' Daddy said, clapping his hands together. 'Let's get on with this. You girls start tidying your rooms, I'm going to fix the computer first to get it out of the way. William D, could you please pick up all the Lego in the playroom?'

'OK,' he said, running off into the house. Daddy watched him go, surprised.

'This parenting thing is easier than I thought,' he said.

I picked up some bowls to take them into the kitchen

and wash them up but I picked up too many and one dropped and smashed.

'Sorry,' I said.

'Never mind,' Daddy replied. 'Just leave the bowls here. I'll wash them up after I've fixed the computer.'

The problem with sorting through old toys is that when you see them you straight away want to start playing with them again. I found my old Polly Pockets that I hadn't had out for months and at first I just thought I'd line them up so I could decide which ones I wanted to keep but then I found myself involved in quite a complicated game. After a bit, Daisy came and joined in. I sometimes wonder if I'm too old for Polly Pockets, but this was a really cool game and quite grown-up. Daisy spent ten minutes looking through the box to find her Polly Pocket, the blonde one with the really long eyelashes. I'm always the one with the short dark hair and the suit. Business Polly, like Mummy used to be.

'How are you getting on with tidying your room?' I asked after a while.

'OK,' Daisy said. 'I haven't really started yet.'

'What have you been doing?'

'First I needed to change into my tidying clothes,' she said. 'Since then, I've been looking at myself in the mirror.'

We played on for a bit but then realised we were getting hungry. I sent Daisy down to find out what was for lunch. She came back a few minutes later.

'Daddy's still fixing the computer and William D is playing with Lego,' she said.

'What about lunch?'

'I think we might need to make it.'

I sighed and went downstairs. Daddy was reading some spreadsheets.

'Shall I make lunch?' I asked.

'Ooh, yes please,' he said, without looking up. So I made sandwiches for everyone. I know what everyone likes. Cheese and hummus for William D; ham, mayonnaise and cucumber for Daisy; chicken, mustard, mayonnaise and tomato for Daddy; cheese and pickle for me. It took ages but eventually we all sat around the table to eat.

'Right,' said Daddy, between mouthfuls. 'It's nearly three o'clock. I think we've made pretty good progress, but we need to step things up a bit. I'm going to find the mower after lunch. I'd like you girls to do the vacuuming. William D, how is the Lego coming along?'

William D had a mouthful of food, so just gave Daddy a big thumbs up.

'Great,' Daddy said. 'Keep working on that.'

It took us quite a long time to find the vacuum and get all the attachments sorted out, but we got most of the hallway done despite William D coming out of the playroom every so often bellowing at us to stop the noise. But then the bag filled up and as we were trying to take it off Daisy dropped it and it went everywhere.

She said it was me who dropped it but it was definitely her. So while Daisy went to find the dustpan and brush I tried to put the bag back on again.

'At least it's empty now,' I said. We managed to get rid of a lot of the pile of dust but I couldn't get the bag back on the vacuum and went to find Daddy to get him to help.

I couldn't see him, so set off through the long grass towards the back. Daisy followed after a moment, stepping daintily so as not to get her nice stripy shoes wet. There are three parts to our back garden. The bit near the house is supposed to be lawn with the kitchen garden on the right and a few bushes on the left – that's lawn one. Then there's a wall and you go through a door into the second part of the garden – lawn two – which is overgrown with trees and bushes and roses that catch at your clothes. There are loads of butterflies and insects which Clematis hunts and eats. The bit at the end of the garden is where there is a greenhouse, some fruit trees and an old veggie patch which has been over-run by brambles. I found Daddy asleep in the greenhouse, listening to the cricket on the portable radio he keeps in there.

'Has he found the mower?' Daisy asked in a whisper, walking up behind me, stepping carefully through the long, damp grass.

'It doesn't look like it,' I said.

'Should we wake him?' she asked.

'No, let's let him snooze for a bit.'

As we went back in I noticed the breakfast things were still on the rusty iron table, covered with ants. The broken bowl was still on the ground. Must remember to bring those in before Mummy gets back, I thought to myself. Then I'm not sure whose idea it was but we decided to watch telly for a while until there was a knock on the door. It was Emily.

'Can I come over and play?' she asked.

'We're supposed to be tidying,' I said, frowning.

'You've got the telly on,' Emily pointed out.

'That's true,' I said. 'We're waiting for Daddy to wake up and help us.'

So Emily came in and we all watched telly together until Daddy came in yawning and asking what time it was.

'Six thirty-five,' Emily said.

'Morning?'

'No, evening,' she said.

'What day?'

'Saturday.'

'Phew!' Daddy said. Then, as if he'd just realised she was there, 'Hello, Emily.'

'Hello,' Emily said, looking at him suspiciously. Emily can be a bit funny around Daddy – I think it's because she doesn't know her daddy very well. Once, as we walked to school together, she asked Mummy what daddies are for.

'That's a good question,' Mummy said, but she didn't try to answer it.

'I mean, I know about the birds and the bees,' Emily said.

'Do you?' Mummy asked, surprised.

'Yes, we learned it all in PSHE.'

'You learned it all?'

'Yes. All of it.'

'Maybe I should do PSHE,' Mummy said. 'There's lots I'm still confused about.'

'Bee colonies keep a few males around, to service the queen,' Emily said. 'They're pretty useless otherwise.'

'Right,' Mummy said. 'Anyway, let's talk about something else . . .'

'And if the food supply runs short they just chuck the males out to die.'

'Oh, that's not very nice,' Mummy said.

'They're expendable. It's Nature's Law,' Emily said fiercely. 'They have no use for the males.'

'What about taking the bins out?' Mummy said. 'Or going downstairs at night to check for burglars?'

'Making spaghetti carbonara?' Daisy suggested.

I think Mummy might have told Daddy about this conversation because whenever Emily's around nowadays he suddenly gets all parenty. It's like he's trying to prove how non-expendable he is. He doesn't want to be chucked out every time we run out of Weetabix.

'Does your mother know you're here?' he asked her.

'Yes,' Emily said.

'Would you like to stay for dinner?' he asked.

'What are we having?'

'Spag bol,' Daddy said. 'And garlic bread.'

I could tell he'd just made this up on the spot. He didn't want to seem disorganised in front of Emily.

'OK,' Emily said. 'Yes please.'

Daddy went off and soon after I could hear him throwing things around in the kitchen so I went to help him find everything. Emily's surname is Bellamy, which Daddy thinks is very funny. I explained to him once that she wasn't always called Emily Bellamy.

'Bellamy is her mummy's surname,' I said. 'When she was born she had her daddy's name but then he got found with all that money in his bank account and had to go to jail. Her mummy asked her if she wanted her name changed to Bellamy and she said yes.'

'What was her father's name?'

'He's not dead.'

'OK. What *is* her father's name,' he corrected.

'Rod,' I said.

'No, his surname,' Daddy said, chopping up some garlic. Daddy cuts up garlic very well. I like to watch him, he's very fast with the knife. It's so sharp and it always gives me a thrill watching him banging it down so fast. Chop, chop, chop.

'Tonk,' I said.

He stopped chopping and looked at me. 'His name is Tonk?'

'Yes, Tonk.'

'Rod Tonk.'

'Yes.'

'Rod Tonk and Emily Tonk.'

'Emily Bellamy now.'

'They're both brilliant names,' he said.

Daddy often sings songs about Emily's name to different tunes, tonight it was to the tune of 'Nellie the Elephant'.

> *Emily Bellamy came to tea*
> *And ate up all the pasta*
> *Bolognese and garlic bread, yum, yum, yum.*

'We haven't got much tidying done,' I said, putting a pan of water on to boil.

'I know,' he said, shaking his head. 'And we've been hard at it ALL DAY.'

He really meant it too. I love Daddy. We all do. And part of the reason we love him is because he's so out of touch with reality. Mummy says he has his head in the clouds. Jacob says he's a dreamer. Daisy says he's silly; William D says he's the best storyteller in the world. Emily says he's a useless drone.

But I can see why Mummy sometimes gets frustrated with him. Sometimes the things you love about a person can also be the things you get cross with them about.

* * *

Daddy said Emily could stay and play after dinner, and by the time she'd gone home, it was too late to do any more tidying or have a bath so we agreed to get up really early in the morning and just 'blitz it'. It's a shame there wasn't time for a bath actually, because after three rounds of Skink Hunt, William D was more than a little grubby.

Usually in our house nobody sleeps late. Here's how things usually work. I wake first and can't get back to sleep. So I go and sit on the window seat and watch the world. Soon after I hear William D's door open and he pads in to see Mummy and Daddy. He doesn't understand about talking quietly in the mornings or closing doors so I hear him telling Mummy and Daddy about Spider-Man or the dream he had about a very rare Pokémon. Then Daddy takes him downstairs so Mummy can have a snooze. The smell of Daddy's morning coffee tiptoes up the stairs and I can hear them crashing about trying to open Front Door to get to the milk bottles. Daisy gets up next and either goes down to watch telly with William D or comes into my room to help me stare out of the window.

Eventually Mummy gets up and tells Daddy off for not giving the children their breakfast yet and then she calls for me to come down for breakfast. I could go down as soon as I hear her get up, I suppose, but I always wait for her to call, just to check she hasn't forgotten about me. She never does.

Today, though, it wasn't like that. Today it wasn't me who woke first, or William D. It was Front Door. Front Door started ringing and banging. I sat up, yawned and stretched and went downstairs to see if I could open her. Today Front Door opened, as if she wanted to see what would happen when she let in the person who was banging and ringing. It turned out to be Mummy.

'Forgot my key,' she said, giving me a cuddle.

'You're back early,' I said.

'It's gone ten,' she replied. 'Anyway, I missed you.'

'I missed you too,' I said.

'I see your father hasn't managed to cut the rhododendron back. How did you get on with the tidying?'

'Err . . .' I said. Together, Mummy and I did a tour of inspection. In the sitting room was Mummy's computer with the back off and a computer manual with approximately one million spreadsheets scattered around the floor. In the hall there was still a big pile of dust which we'd forgotten to sweep up from the vacuum. In the playroom the floor was covered with Lego and DVD cases. In the kitchen the washing-up was sitting in the sink, as was Clematis, who looked up at us briefly before getting back to licking the pan with the Bolognese sauce in. Mummy went to the back door and looked out at yesterday's breakfast things on the table and at the grass, longer than ever.

Upstairs Mummy looked in my room and saw the Polly Pockets all over the floor and the bin-liner she'd given me for the toys still lying on the floor, empty.

'And Daisy's room?' she asked.

'Same as mine,' I replied, looking at the floor.

'So you haven't done any of the things I asked you to do?'

'No.'

'OK,' she said. 'Why don't you go downstairs and fix yourself some breakfast?'

'Where are you going?'

'I'm going to go and have a word with your father,' she said, in a cold voice. As she passed I saw her earlobes had gone white.

I swallowed. Poor Daddy, I thought, then scurried off downstairs.

Later on that day I crept up to my little room and wrote more of the My House report. I wanted to write about the kitchen. It's probably the most important room in the house because that's where we spend most of our time.

SCHOOL LUNCH REPORT

Day: Mon, Tue, Wed, Thu, Fri

Child's Name: William D

Class: Caterpillars

Today your child:

Hardly ate any food

- Ate no food

Details: He says he is left-handed and needs a special left-handed spoon. Please phone the office.

Signed:

Mrs Gurney

School Secretary

The Kitchen

Our kitchen is big and full. It was the room Mummy really loved when we first came to look at the house, though you could see a whole lot more of the garden from the kitchen door back then because the grass was neatly cut. There's an Aga, which makes the whole room cosy in the winter. There's a radio that is always on Radio 4, which is usually really boring but sometimes they talk about a politician who's been caught with a lady who's not his wife, which is always fun to listen to. Sometimes on the news they talk about people being horribly murdered and Mummy sings loudly during those bits so we can't hear the details.

The fridge is covered with photos and drawings we've all done and fridge magnets from holidays in Dorset and William D's star chart and the latest note he's brought back from school.

Since William D found out that left-handed people sometimes find things difficult with tools designed for right-handed people, he uses it as an excuse not to be able to do anything. Mummy says she blames herself for buying him special left-handed scissors. When he had to draw a square at school he insisted he needed a left-handed ruler. When Daddy was trying to teach him to ride he said he needed a left-handed bicycle.

It's odd, because he's quite happy using a right-handed mouse when he plays computer games. But Mummy took a normal spoon out of the cupboard and wrote L on it with an indelible marker and put it in William D's school bag.

I like the kitchen more than any other room except my own room. It's because the kitchen is the room we spend most of the time together in. Even though it's not that big and can get very crowded and a bit noisy when everyone's arguing or chatting and the radio is on and the dishwasher's running.

The cats like the kitchen too. They each have a basket next to the Aga where it's warm. They never go in different baskets, they always squash in together even though there's not enough room for two fully-grown cats.

'I wonder why they do that?' Daddy asked once, leaning down and scratching Clematis on the chin. 'You can have your very own basket, you silly cat. It'd be much more comfortable.'

But I knew the answer.

'They like being together more than they like being comfortable,' I told him.

Mad Tamsin

Mad Tamsin came over for a play date the next day. Mad Tamsin is Daisy's best friend and she's called Mad Tamsin because her name is Tamsin and . . . well, she's madder than a tent peg, as Daisy would say. She's really lovely and everyone likes her, but Mummy dreads her visits as she is very adventurous and extremely accident-prone. She especially loves to climb on things. Tables, bookshelves, trees, the side of the house. It's like she swallowed a balloon when she was a baby and it's always forcing her upwards, as high as she can go.

One time, we were at the wall-climbing centre and the instructor was giving us this really boring talk about safety and Tamsin just went ahead and climbed up the wall behind him without a safety harness and then couldn't get down and they had to get a ladder. Last December she tried to climb up the Christmas tree and pulled it over on top of herself.

Even when she's not climbing she somehow manages to get herself into trouble.

When she came camping with us her hair went on fire when we were toasting marshmallows. Another time she went to London with her family and got on the wrong train and went to Basingstoke on her own and made friends with a DJ in a wheelchair who let her call her mummy on his mobile phone. He also bought her some crisps and gave her one of his music CDs. The British Transport Police had to bring her back. She's still got the CD.

She always has a big smile on her face though, and when she does something daft she says, 'What am I like? What am I like?'

Her parents do it too, they grin and roll their eyes and say, 'What is she like? What is she like?'

Mummy was out at the gym and so the rest of us played BOOMball, which is usually only mildly dangerous but Tamsin managed somehow to get the elastic string wrapped around her neck. Later she climbed up onto the rusty iron table to get into a better fielding position. It immediately collapsed in a shower of rusty flakes and she hurt her ankle.

'Are you OK?' Daddy asked, helping her up.

'Yes, fine,' she said, grinning and limping. 'What am I like?'

When it was Daddy's turn to be The Boomer, he hit the ball so hard the elasticated string snapped and it sailed down to the end of the garden into The Thicket.

'Shot!' Daddy said.

'Daddy!' we shouted, crossly.

'Don't worry, don't worry, I'll get it.' He ran down to

The Thicket but then stopped and peered in, nervously. We all followed him and stood just behind. The Thicket is dark and gloomy. None of us is really sure how far back it goes because it's so overgrown. Clematis sometimes goes in and comes back with wildlife in his mouth but The Slug won't go in at all.

'It's thick in there,' I said.

'Thick as a toothbrush,' Daisy said.

'William D,' Daddy said. 'Do you think you could squeeze in and find the ball?'

'No way,' William D said.

'What about one of you girls?' Daddy suggested.

'I'll go,' Tamsin said. She doesn't care about anything.

'No. Not you,' Daddy said. 'You'll be bitten by a spider, or eaten by an anaconda or something. I don't want to have to explain to your mother why all your bones have been crushed by an Amazonian reptile.'

'You hit it in there,' Daisy said. 'You should go.'

'I don't want to,' Daddy said. 'It's all wet and yucky and there are spiders and creepy crawlies. I think you should go, Chloe.'

'OK,' I said straight away.

'What? Are you sure?' Daddy asked.

'Yes, I'm sure,' I said. I took a deep breath and stepped forward. I held out a hand and pushed the leaves of a bush aside. Then I walked into The Thicket. Daddy was right. It was wet, it was yucky, and there *were* spiders. But I was brave. It wasn't really the ball I wanted, I just wanted to be the first one to explore. I can be quite determined when I set my mind to it. I pushed forward, shivering as a wet leaf dragged itself across my neck and dripped rainwater down my back. Past the first row of overgrown bushes there was another rhododendron, even bigger than the one at the side of the house. I stepped over a couple of thick branches, so heavy they had sunk nearly to ground level. Inside the rhododendron it was dry and I could stand up without my head touching the leaves.

'Are you OK?' I heard Daddy call. 'We can't see you any more.'

'I'm fine,' I called back peering around in the gloom. 'There's another rhododendron in here, and I think I can see an apple tree, and . . . and . . .'

'What?' Daddy cried. 'What is it? Are you OK?'

But I didn't answer him immediately. I'd seen something beyond the rhododendron. It looked like a wall, made of wood. A shed?

'Chloe?'

'I can see something made of wood,' I said. 'I'm going to investigate.'

'A tree?' Daddy suggested. What a comedian. 'There's a wooden door,' I called. 'I'm going in.'

'Is it a wardrobe?' Daddy shouted. 'Can you see Mr Tumnus?'

I pulled the door open with difficulty and went inside. It wasn't a shed, I could see that immediately. It was a summerhouse; dark inside with all the tangled bushes pressed up against the windows. Brambles had crept in through the cracks in the boards and there was a wasps' nest in the eaves, but it didn't look rotten.

'Chloe?' Daddy called again.

'You've GOT to come and see,' I said.

Curiosity got the better of them and soon after Daddy came rustling through the leaves, saying rude words under his breath.

'WOW!' Daisy said when she saw the summerhouse.

'Awkward!' William D added. 'What is it?'

'It's a summerhouse,' Daddy said. 'Looks in good condition apart from the wasps' nest.'

'WASPS!' William D shouted. 'Cool!'

'I suppose the rhododendron kept it nice and dry,' Daddy said. 'The question is what do we do with it now?'

'We could clean it,' Daisy said. 'And use it for a secret clubhouse.'

'We could cut the bushes back, get rid of the brambles,' Daddy suggested. 'Bring a radio and a hammock.'

'We could breed a wasp army,' William D said. 'And rule the universe.'

I was about to tell them my idea, when we heard something on the roof. Something big and heavy, moving around. We looked at each other in fear.

'The anaconda,' Daddy said, laughing, but I could tell he was puzzled.

'Wasp Queen,' William D said confidently. Daddy went outside and peered up at the roof.

'Careful, Daddy,' I said.

'I thought I told you to wait outside,' Daddy said to someone on the roof.

'It's Tamsin!' Daisy said, suddenly realising. We all rushed outside to see Tamsin on the roof grinning at us.

'It's brilliant up here,' she said. 'You can climb up on this big tree.'

'I think you should come down now,' Daddy said.

'It's not dangerous,' Tamsin said, walking around. 'Look, it's all perfectly . . . aaargh!'

Suddenly, with that shriek, she disappeared from view. Daddy ran around the other side.

'She's gone over the fence,' he said. 'Tamsin, are you OK?'

'I'm fine,' she said. 'I landed in something soft. Some plants. I'll climb back over.'

'No!' Daddy yelled. 'No more climbing. You're in Mr Coleman's garden, go to the front and I'll meet you there. If Mr Coleman sees you, don't tell him you came from our garden. He's still cross with us about the bonfire incident.'

We all rushed to the front to meet Tamsin only to find Mr Coleman had captured her and had brought her to Front Door. Front Door wouldn't open so Daddy popped his head out of the window to talk to Mr Coleman.

'One of yours?' Mr Coleman asked.

'Temporarily,' Daddy said, cheerfully.

'She landed in my tomatoes,' Mr Coleman said. 'Ruined them.'

'Sorry about that,' Daddy said. 'I'm going to Tesco later, I can get some for you.'

'I don't like the ones from Tesco,' Mr Coleman said. 'They're full of pesticides. I only put organic products on my tomatoes.'

'Well, what's more organic than an eight-year-old girl?' Daddy asked. He was really trying to be friendly but Mr Coleman gave him A Look.

'You know, it was quiet in this street before you came,' he said to Daddy.

'You mean dull,' Daddy replied.

'No,' Mr Coleman said. 'I mean quiet.' And with that he turned and stormed off as Daddy dragged Tamsin in through the window.

Mummy came back from the gym soon after and it was time for dinner. Between us, Tamsin and I broke two plates and a glass. So we had to abandon the summerhouse for the evening. Daddy promised we'd try and clear a path to it on the weekend, then we'd decide what we'd use it for. While we were eating Clematis brought something in from the garden and dropped it at Mummy's feet. Something furry.

Mummy squealed, leaping backwards. 'John!'

'Sweeeeet,' Daisy said.

'Aww sweeeee—' Tamsin began.

'It's dead,' I said, peering at it.

'Thanks, Clematis,' Mummy said. 'Thanks very much for this dead mouse.' She was being sarcastic. Daddy peered at the poor little creature.

'It's a vole, actually,' he said.

'Thanks for the Natural History lesson, David Attenborough,' Mummy said. 'Now can you get rid of it?'

Daddy picked up the tiny creature with some newspaper and took it to the bins. Daisy was sad about the little vole.

'Cats are hunters,' I explained. 'Voles are prey. It's Nature's Law.'

'A bit too much of Nature's Law around here if you ask me,' Mummy said. 'It's the third murder we've had this week. It's teeming with Nature out there.'

When Daddy came back in Mummy grabbed him by the shoulders and said, 'Mow the lawn. Or I will divorce you.'

She was only joking. I think.

Part Three

The Garden

I think the real reason Daddy doesn't ever do any work in the garden is because he actually likes it being wild. In the summer the middle lawn becomes a mass of wildflowers. Daisy and I picked some and brought them in. Mummy helped us look up their names on the iPad. The blue ones are cornflowers, the red ones are poppies and the yellow ones are buttercups. The white ones are daisies and those are Daisy's favourite, of course. In the summer there are thousands of butterflies everywhere and the occasional droning bee, going from flower to flower, as busy as a mummy. Or as busy as a jam jar, Daisy might say.

It's the perfect garden for cats. They've always got somewhere to hide and stalk through the long grass, pouncing on innocent little creatures. Daisy gets upset when they kill things and, if I'm honest, so do I but I know about wildlife and understand that it's Nature's Law for Clematis to leave bits of starling under the TV cabinet.

Soon after we got the cats, Mummy spent a lot of

time looking on the internet about how to look after them and what to do if they wouldn't eat and what to do if they did eat but only baby birds and slugs. One of the things she learned was that you had to make a distinctive noise when it was time for their dinner, preferably high-pitched. So the first time we fed them Mummy went out the back and tried to think of something distinctive. The conversation went like this.

'What should I call?' she asked me and Daisy.

'What about their names?' Daisy said.

'The Slug? I can't call out The Slug,' she said. 'Or Clematis. "The Slug, The Slug! Clematis!" People will think I've gone mad.'

'People already think you're mad,' Daddy said.

'What about DINNER TIME! DINNER TIME!?' I said.

'The website says best not to use the word dinner, or else every time they hear that word they'll think it's for them.'

'What words did the website suggest you use?' Daddy asked.

'Anything, it doesn't even need to be words,' Mummy said. 'As long as it's the same sound every night.'

Eventually she ran out of patience and just went 'DOOBY-DOOBY-DOO!!' in a piercing voice. They came and now every night one of us has to go out the back and yell 'DOOBY-DOOBY-DOO!!' at the top of our voice.

Daddy tried to do it in a deep voice and it didn't work. The cats don't come unless you shriek it.

Daddy sighed and asked why she'd chosen DOOBY-DOOBY-DOO!! and Mummy pointed out she hadn't heard any brilliant ideas from him.

There's a sort of path through the middle section of the garden, which isn't a proper path with paving stones or anything but just the bit where we always walk. That leads to the greenhouse and The Thicket at the back, all dark and tangled. I often see Daddy walking up and down, 'inspecting his estate', as he calls it. He's always smiling when he's in the garden.

I remember one day last year we walked around together on one of these inspections and he told me about all his plans for the garden that he hasn't actually got around to doing. It must have been autumn then because I remember the trees and bushes were a hundred different shades of brown and red and russet and yellow and still a little green. There were squashy Bramleys under the apple tree and when you stepped on them they smelled like cider and vinegar and apple pie. In London we weren't allowed to have fires but in autumn in Weyford there is always smoke coming out of chimneys and people burning dead branches and leaves in their back gardens. So in October and November there is always the lovely smell of wood smoke on York Road.

Whenever I smell wood smoke I think of my daddy in the garden, smiling.

I love our garden, even if it's a bit messy, and I love my daddy even if his plans are bigger than his efforts. Sometimes, though, I wish he'd try a bit harder. Just to make Mummy smile, too.

Imogen

It turned out none of us had seen Jacob since he left for his date with Charlie on Friday night. Mummy was cross at Daddy about this.

'I go away for one night and you lose one of the children,' she said.

'He always turns up eventually,' Daddy said. 'But since he never tidies his room, it's hard to tell if he's been sleeping there or not.'

On Tuesday after school Mummy texted Jacob.

'Are you alive?' Mummy read out as she typed. We were at the Maltings, the big building next to the river where they have theatre and the Beer Festival that Daddy always goes to and where Daisy does ballet and I do my Modern and Tap. I'd finished my lesson but Daisy's didn't finish for another half an hour. We always hang around in the coffee shop until she's done. Mummy has a coffee and gets me an orange juice and William D gets a babyccino, which he never finishes but instead runs around annoying other customers. He's always really tired after school and is even more William D than usual.

'So how was school?' she asked, putting the phone

down. She gave me the look that means she's worried about me. She says she always knows when things aren't good at school because I don't sleep very well. I don't always tell her if Imogen's been horrible to me at school. And it's hard to know what to say really. It's not like she's pinching me or pushing me over in the hall. She just doesn't include me in games and if I go and stand with Imogen's gang they just ignore me or move away, whispering and looking back at me and laughing. But the crazy thing is that they only do that when Imogen's there. When she's not they're OK. Hannah is quite friendly when Imogen's not there. The whole thing is stupid.

So I go to find Emily and play with her and that's fine but then Mummy asks who I played with and if I say just Emily she says, 'Sweetie, I wish you'd expand your circle of friends. Emily's a good friend but she's a little possessive.' And I say, I'll try tomorrow.

Sometimes I try to play with Tobias because he's always on his own too but he's difficult to play with properly and he doesn't always understand the game and gets upset about nothing and runs off all red-faced and shouting. Today I found a quiet spot and just got on with reading my book.

'School was good,' I said. But I was lying a bit. I like school when I'm in class. I love Mrs Fuller and I like my table, because everyone knows it's the table for the clever people even though you're not supposed to know and I get on well with Thomas and Oliver when we're working on maths problems together. But at break the boys all run off and play football and girls aren't invited even though Daddy says I've got a really good kick. But if I say all this to Mummy then she'll call up the school to say I'm not fitting in and I'm being bullied and why aren't I allowed to play football and Mrs Fuller will try to organise our play so that everyone's included but Imogen and Sophie and Hannah and the others always know what's going on. And the boys will get annoyed because they have to play a really rubbish game of football without tackling. They'll all go along with it for that day then the next day it's back to how it was before except even worse because the girls all know it was about me. And let's face it, no one will want to come to my party if I go around telling tales.

'Are you sure?' Mummy said. 'Because I heard you shouting in your sleep last night.'

'I was dreaming William D fell down a well,' I said, lying. I didn't like lying to Mummy, but I didn't want to tell her I was worried about my party after she'd agreed we could have it in the garden.

'We should be so lucky,' Mummy said, watching him re-write the menu on the little blackboard by the cash register. She was just joking though. I'm almost positive Mummy doesn't really want William D to fall down a well. She was about to get up and drag him away when her phone buzzed and she snatched it up.

'It's Jacob,' she said, reading the screen. Her face fell.

'What does it say?' I asked.

'It says "Who is this?"' Mummy replied. Then she texted back.

There was a crash from near the till. William D had knocked over a stand of gingerbread men and was acting like it wasn't anything to do with him. I went over to collect him and apologise to the man who made the coffee. He shrugged.

'That's OK, I'm used to it.'

'Yes, I suppose you must be,' I said, looking around. Everyone in there was either a tired-looking mummy or a tired-looking child.

'He's not the only little terror who knocks over the stands,' the man said, grinning.

'Though he has done it three times today,' I pointed out. I dragged the protesting William D back to Mummy's table. She was reading another text from Jacob.

'He says he lost all the contacts off his phone,' she said. 'I'm not sure I believe him.'

'Why would he make that up?' I asked.

'So he has a good excuse to not answer,' she said. 'If one of his girlfriends phones, he can say he didn't pick up because he thought she was someone trying to sell him insurance.'

I was about to ask Mummy about the party when there was another huge crash from the counter. We peered over to see William D had got himself tangled up in a rack of snack foods and knocked the whole lot over.

Mummy sighed. 'Do you think we could pretend he's nothing to do with us and just leave?'

'No,' I said. 'I think we're stuck with him.'

The next day we were doing maths and Mrs Fuller put Imogen on my table. I usually like maths, not just because I like maths but because of the other people on my table. It's usually Thomas and Oliver and Hannah and we all laugh together, especially when Thomas does his impression of Taylor Swift doing the speaking bit in 'We Are Never Ever Getting Back Together'. But today Oliver and a few other people were ill and Mrs Fuller moved us around so we had groups of four. We got Imogen. Great.

It didn't take long before she started being horrid. We were supposed to be discussing a problem we'd been set but she started talking about her party instead.

'Are you looking forward to my party, Hannah?' she said.

Hannah did look a bit embarrassed because she knew I wasn't invited but she said she was.

'We're having a live band,' Imogen said. 'And a hog roast.'

Even Thomas looked interested. I knew Imogen was only talking about it to annoy me. And it was working.

'I don't think it's polite to talk about a party in front of people who aren't invited,' I said.

'Sorry I couldn't invite you, Chloe,' Imogen said. 'Daddy said I was only allowed to have fifty people.'

'Not me,' I said. 'I meant Thomas.'

Imogen blinked in surprise. No one invited boys to their party.

'Are any boys invited to your party?' I asked her, innocently. She shook her head. I think she suddenly realised that this made her look like a baby. She pretended to be all grown-up but didn't really have any friends who were boys.

'If I have a party,' I said. 'I'm going to invite the boys too.'

There was a silence after that. Thomas grabbed the paper and studied it hard. I felt my face going red. I hadn't meant to embarrass him, just to shut Imogen up for a bit. But suddenly everything had got a bit complicated. It wasn't just about the timing, or that I was worried about the state of the house. Now I was worried about having to invite boys like I'd said I was going to. I'd really quite like to invite Oliver and Thomas because I like them and they're nice to me. The other day Thomas told me a joke and I laughed so hard I snorted and that set Oliver off and the three of us rolled about laughing for ages. I saw Imogen giving me evils after that, like I'm not allowed to have friends who are boys. So I want to invite them but I don't think they'll come because they'll think it's weird that a girl has asked them to her party and everyone will say I want them to be my boyfriends. Which I don't.

But if I did want one of them to be my boyfriend it would be Thomas.

It would be much simpler if I just invited a few people to go ice-skating and then for pizza. Emily, Tamsin, Daisy and maybe Hattie and Hannah. Going for pizza is a good option because people's parents tend to turn up to the pizza bit and they drink beer and wine down one end of the table and talk loudly and just let us get on with things, which means we can stay longer and keep ordering food and fizzy drinks.

I'd prefer a big party though.

The Spare Room/
Daisy's Room

Daisy's room is bigger than mine but I don't mind. She has a very big mirror in it that she uses A LOT. She practises her ballet in front of it. She practises her singing in front of it. She tries on different outfits in front of it – one time I even caught her practising crying in front of the mirror. She said she was rehearsing for a play but I think she just wanted to see what she looks like when she cries.

When Daisy grows up, she wants to be an optician. Or a ballerina. Or an IT person who does useful things, or a lawyer like Mummy. Even though Mummy says being a lawyer is the worst job in the world, Daisy doesn't really believe her.

You can see the back garden from Daisy's room, and also you can see into Mr Coleman's garden. Mr Coleman is the neighbour whose house is attached to ours and Justin and Gavin are our neighbours-the-other-way. We go into Daisy's room when we want to watch what's going on out the back. We go into my room when we want to watch what's going on out the front. It's a good arrangement.

We do argue sometimes, of course. Daisy doesn't mind what order she watches programmes in which drives me mad because you're supposed to start from the beginning and watch each programme in order or else it doesn't make as much sense and you see spoilers. She says I take it too seriously but actually it's Daisy who doesn't take it seriously enough!

Daisy and I also have a long-running dispute over who owns Dirty Millie. Dirty Millie is a rag doll with one eye that used to belong to Mummy and Mummy gave it to me when I was tiny. Daisy says that Mummy gave it to her, which is such rubbish because I already HAD Dirty Millie when Daisy was born so how could Mummy have given it to her? I asked Mummy and she said she couldn't remember giving it to either of us and that she had a headache and if we didn't stop fighting over it she'd take it away. Now we take it in turns to have Dirty Millie for a week but sometimes Daisy keeps her for longer because I forget, and then when I try to keep her for longer to make up for it Daisy comes and steals her and we start fighting again. But quietly, in case Mummy does take Dirty Millie.

Daisy is convinced there is a ghost in the house. She thinks it lives in the spare room most of the time but sometimes walks up and down the stairs at night moaning and clanking chains. I always tell her she's being silly, but sometimes I get a shivery feeling when I walk past the spare room. It's completely her fault for filling my head full of these ideas.

Directly under Daisy's room is the spare room. Even though there are no such things as ghosts, the spare room feels like it should be haunted. It's creepy in there, the floorboards creak even more than in other parts of the house. The radiator groans and clanks and never seems to warm the air; I told Daisy that this is what she can hear when she hears the 'ghost' in the night but she doesn't believe me. The spare room is small, on the first floor, next to the family bathroom, and its window looks out over the back garden. Most of the light is blocked by a big old tree just outside. It's Granny Jean's room when she comes to stay. When she's there the room seems warm and cosy and we love to go in. But when it's empty we stay out.

But there's definitely no ghost.

Milk School

I lay in bed that night thinking about Imogen and how mean she was. I think school would be perfect if only she wasn't there. Or if she suddenly decided to start being nice, but that was about as likely as Daddy mowing the lawn. Everything would be perfect if it wasn't for Imogen. And if Front Door would open when we wanted it to. And if I could find Sylvia the snail, who was still missing. My little clock with the illuminated hands said it was 4.47 when I heard a little noise from outside. Just a tiny little clink. But I knew straight away what it was. I jumped out of bed and ran across to the window. Down in the street below I saw the white roof of Cara's milk float, pale in the darkness.

I rushed downstairs as quietly as I could. I could hear Daddy snoring on the first floor but Mummy is a light sleeper and sometimes gets up in the middle of the night.

I didn't even try Front Door but opened the window in the sitting room and leaped across onto the steps, just as Cara was setting down our milk bottles. She jumped a mile and clutched her chest but managed to avoid shrieking at least.

'Chloe!' she hissed. 'You *have* to stop doing that. You nearly gave me a heart attack!'

'Sorry,' I said. 'I heard you outside and I was awake, so I thought I'd come and say hello.'

'You heard me?'

'Yes.'

'Either you have amazing ears or I'm losing my touch,' Cara said.

'Can I ride on your float again?'

Cara rubbed her chin, thinking about this.

'Did you tell your parents about the last time?'

'Yes,' I lied.

'And your Mum, she said it was OK?'

I nodded.

'All right, hop on. You can tell me the gossip.'

As soon as I was on the float with Cara, I started talking. I told her all about Imogen and how I always ended up playing with Emily, because Imogen was always at the centre of the group of girls I wanted to play with. Cara nodded and shushed me sometimes when I got too excited and forgot to whisper.

'Sorry,' I said. 'I think I'm too much of a chatterbox to be a good milk-lady.'

'It takes years of practise. It's harder than you'd think to learn quietness. Do you know, a lot of milkmen and women go to work in libraries when they leave the job?' Cara told me. 'There are similar skills required. Being quiet and telling other people to be quiet, for example.'

140

'Transferable skills,' I muttered.

'That's right,' she said. 'Transferable skills.'

Cara let me deliver some bottles on my own again. Not everyone on York Street had milk delivered, of course, but Cara had to drive right down the other end to make sure Mr Thoreau had his grapefruit juice. I did Mrs Groves at number 38, the Jones's at 44 and Mrs Simpson at number 62. Mrs Simpson had just the one bottle.

'She used to have two bottles,' Cara said, 'just after she got married the last time. But she's dropped back to one.'

'I hope Mr Simpson's all right,' I said. 'No one's seen him for ages.'

Cara shrugged. 'One thing you learn in this job is that people come and go. Especially if they're married to Mrs Simpson.'

'So what do you think I should do about Imogen?'

'I used to be bullied,' Cara said.

'You?!'

'Shhh,' she said.

'Sorry. It's just that you're so lovely. Why would anyone bully you?'

'Hey,' she said. 'You're lovely too, OK? You're not being bullied because there's something wrong with you. Always remember that. It's something wrong with the bully instead.'

'OK,' I said.

I was amazed that anyone would have the nerve to bully Cara, who was quite tall and strong. She could lift three milk crates at once. But I didn't say that. We had to stop the conversation then as Cara went off to deliver two semi-skimmed bottles to the Fletchers.

'Who bullied you?' I asked when she got back.

She put the float into gear and it hummed as we moved off. 'Some idiot. At milk school,' she said.

'I didn't know there was a milk school,' I said.

'Of course there's a milk school,' she said. 'They have schools for butchers and bakers, don't they?'

'Yes,' I said, even though I wasn't sure that they did.

Cara went on. 'Anyway, there was another girl there and I thought we might be friends, because there weren't many girls who wanted to deliver milk in those days. Not seriously.'

'But she didn't want to be friends?'

'No. She wanted to be mean to me and make me feel bad,' Cara said. 'It took me a long time before I found out why.'

'Why?' I asked. But I had to wait again to find out as Cara and I had to hop off the float again to make deliveries on either side of the road.

'One day I walked right up to her and said that we needed to talk,' Cara said. 'I made her go for a coffee with me, away from all the men, away from the classroom.'

'You had a classroom?'

'Don't interrupt,' Cara said. 'I sat her down and made her tell me why she was bullying me.'

'What did she say?'

'At first she said she wasn't bullying me. That all the names she called me were just jokes. "Banter," she said. But when I told her how it made me feel she became upset. When it was just me and her she was different. She had no audience to perform in front of. Eventually she told me she felt scared and out of place. She'd never been good at anything, except bullying people, and when she saw how confident I was, even in this man's world, she felt scared of me, so she started making jokes and mean comments to defend herself.'

'She said all that?' I asked, thinking of how Imogen liked to surround herself with a group of girls who laughed at all her jokes. Was Imogen scared? Not of me, surely?

'Not in so many words,' Cara said as she hefted a crate of milk bottles to one side, hardly clinking at all. 'But that was the general idea. Bullies are all the same. They're frightened. If you stand up to them they back down. Often they're people who've been bullied themselves, maybe by their parents.'

'And you think Imogen's like that?'

'Maybe,' Cara said. She stopped the float and got out before turning back to face me. 'Or maybe she's just a right little cow.'

I covered my open mouth with my hand, shocked and delighted that Cara had said 'cow'.

'Thanks for helping today,' Cara said as she dropped me off outside our house. 'And thanks for the talk. I hope it all works out at school.'

When I got in I made myself some breakfast and sat in the quiet kitchen, looking out at the wildflowers in the garden. The Slug jumped up into my lap and let me stroke him for a while. As I sat there, munching my Cheerios, I made a decision. And when Mummy came down I told her that I do want a party even if lots of people can't come. We wrote invitations together and I asked her about Thomas and Oliver and she said we should DEFINITELY invite them.

Daddy came in as I licked the last envelope and sealed it. He yawned and patted my head as he joined me in looking out of the window at the garden. He sighed happily and sang.

> *Spring has sprung,*
> *The grass is ris.*
> *I wonder where the birdies is?*

'Clematis has eaten them,' Mummy said.

After breakfast we took the invitations in to school and Mummy handed them out to the other mummies at the school gate. I hung around to watch as she gave them to Oliver and Thomas's mummies, who seemed surprised but pleased.

Imogen came up to me at lunchtime with Hannah and Sophie tagging along behind, whispering to each other and giggling.

'Did you invite Thomas and Oliver to your party?' she asked.

'Yes,' I said. I could feel my cheeks going red.

'Do you like them?' she asked.

'Yes,' I said. 'They're not mean to me like *some* people.'

'Well, I just heard them talking to the other boys about it and they think it's weird that you asked them.' She put on a concerned face, as though she was telling me some important information she thought I should know, like a friend would. I'm pretty sure she was lying though. I could tell from her face.

I didn't know what to say.

'Also, Greta can't make it,' Imogen said. 'She'll be in Morocco.' Then they went off. Later on, Emily said that she'd heard from Hattie that Thomas and Oliver HADN'T said they thought it was weird they were invited, but actually that IMOGEN had told them it was weird and it was only after that they got embarrassed.

How does Imogen know who I invited? Why does she care anyway? I was so cross I couldn't concentrate on my schoolwork that afternoon and Mrs Fuller frowned at me when she asked me a question and I couldn't answer. Also, Thomas and Oliver hardly talked to me. They seemed a bit embarrassed. It had been a mistake to invite them, I should have known Imogen would stir up trouble.

I was a bit miserable when I got home, but then Mummy reminded me it was the School Fair tomorrow and that cheered me up a bit.

ST ANDREW'S INFANT SCHOOL

SCHOOL LUNCH REPORT

Day: Mon, Tue, Wed, Thu, Fri

Child's Name: William D

Class: Caterpillars

Today your child:

- Hardly ate any food
- Ate no food

Details: William D had a 'misadventure' with his tray.

Signed: Mrs Gurney

School Secretary

School Council

Later on, while Mummy was making dinner, Daddy came into the room unexpectedly and gave her a fright.

She squealed and punched him on the arm in annoyance.

'Sorry,' he said, trying not to laugh.

'William D has some news,' she said to him when she'd recovered.

'Oh, what's that?' Daddy asked. But William D was suddenly too shy to say so Mummy had to explain that William D has been made a representative on the School Council. Daddy raised an eyebrow.

'Yes,' Mummy said. 'I was surprised as well.'

'How did this come about?' Daddy asked William D.

'There was voting,' William D said. 'There were three people from our class who got voted. Shaynala got eight votes, Eliza got six votes and I got five votes. Oscar voted for me and all the Williams and George because I gave him a Pokémon card.'

'That's only nineteen votes,' Mummy said. 'There are thirty in your class.'

'Harry and Dylan got three each,' said William D,

counting on his fingers. 'Zach and Meera got two each and Leon got one, but only because he voted for himself even though you weren't allowed.'

'You split the vote,' Daddy said. 'Nice work.'

'Thanks,' William D said. 'I was the only William to get any votes. I told William P I was going to vote for him but I didn't.'

Mummy hopes the result might be good for him and help him learn to be more responsible but I'm not convinced. The day before he'd brought home yet ANOTHER School Lunch Report.

'Misadventure?' Mummy said. 'What does that mean?'

William D shrugged so Mummy had to phone the school to find out. Apparently William D and Oscar were messing around putting their lunch trays on their heads and there was a certain amount of spillage.

'Do you know how much I pay for your school lunches?' she asked.

'How much?'

'Seventy-two pounds per term,' Mummy said.

'Is that a lot?' he asked.

'Forty-two pence per day,' I said. I remembered this because we had to work it out in maths when I was in Year Two. I have a good memory for things like that.

'Actually, when you put it like that it doesn't sound very much,' Mummy admitted. 'But you must start eating your lunch, William D. I don't want any more of these notes.'

'Sorry, Mummy,' William D said.

'Never mind sorry,' she said. 'Think of the star chart. Think of the Pokémon toy that could be yours.'

The Fair

The next day it was the school's Summer Fair. We were very excited because we were getting five pounds each to spend and we were allowed to have a sausage sandwich and a fizzy drink for lunch. Mummy read us the riot act before we went because we disgraced ourselves last year.

Firstly William D stole a coconut from the coconut shy, ran off with it and hid in the girls loos so Daddy couldn't follow him. Then Daisy went on the bouncy castle and when she got off she accidentally put on another girl's shoes. Daddy went missing and we eventually found him in the beer tent with his friends. Finally I fell off the back of the tractor ride and hurt my wrist. It was my fault because you aren't supposed to stand up and Mummy had to take me to the first aid tent which meant she missed the end of the Silent Auction and didn't get the hour-long massage at Ruby's Rubs she'd been bidding on.

'It went for seven pounds!' she'd said. 'I was willing to pay twice that.'

We all promised to be on our best behaviour and held out our hands as Mummy put five shiny, heavy pound-coins on our palms. William D dropped his straight away so Mummy put them in her pocket for safekeeping. But Daisy and I had little shoulder bags that Granny Jean had brought back for us from Venice. We put our money in those.

We met up with Emily and her mummy and walked to the school with them. William D ran off ahead and we charged after him, saying we were going to keep an eye on him but really we just wanted to run and feel the wind in our faces. The gardens we passed on the street were all beautifully neat, with flowers bursting the beds; the lawns were neatly mown and the paths all clean and with sharp edges. Not like our garden.

When we got to the school it was spitting a bit with rain.

'It always rains for the School Fair,' Vicky said gloomily.

We didn't care though and Emily and I ran off to look at all the stands and games and things. We had a go on the coconut shy, and the lucky dip, and the tombola, and the bouncy castle and the tractor pull. Though it wasn't really a tractor, just a ride-on mower with the blade taken off, pulling a car trailer. We ran out of money very quickly and went to find Mummy, hoping she'd give us some more. I knew where she'd be, floating around the silent auction. When she saw me she beckoned me over.

'I've got the top bid on a new iPhone,' said Mummy, whispering. 'There are two and I think most people haven't realised. Everyone's bidding on Lot 6 but Lot 12 is the other iPhone and that sheet's a bit hidden.'

'Did you hide it?' I asked.

'WHAT?!' she said, shaking her head at my accusation. 'How *could* you think that? It's for charity.'

'Sorry,' I said. 'Should I put the sheet somewhere where people can see it?'

'No need for that,' she said quickly. 'But you could do me a favour? William D is doing my head in, could you go and take him to see the fire engine?'

'OK,' I said. So Emily and I went with William D to see the fire brigade exhibition. Little kids were lining up to sit in the cab and try on a helmet. A lady firefighter was answering questions.

'No, I've never seen a person burn to death.'

'Yes, I have carried a man down a ladder over my shoulder.'

'No, he wasn't naked.'

'Yes, I've had to cut the top off a crashed car.'

'No, I've never had to drop a baby out of a window into someone's arms.'

William D was nearly sick with excitement by the time we got to the front of the queue. He sprang up the steps without any help, clapped on the helmet and started pressing buttons on a computer screen in the cab.

'Err, should he be doing that?' Emily asked.

The lady firefighter looked. 'He can't do any damage, it's in safe mode.'

William D kept furiously stabbing buttons. I tried to think of a good question.

'Did you have to go to Fire School?' I asked her, thinking of Cara at Milk School.

'I trained to be a firefighter, yes,' the lady said. 'I . . .'

But she was interrupted by the wail of a siren. She spun in alarm to find William D had somehow overridden the safe mode and had turned on the lights and siren. As we watched, he pulled a cord dangling down and the fire engine made a booming fog horn noise that made everyone at the fair leap out of their socks and rattled the windows in the school building fifty yards away. The firefighter reached over and turned it off. Everyone was looking at us now. Our ears were ringing. I've never seen William D look happier.

'How the heck did he do that?' she asked, astonished. Except she said a grown-up word instead of heck.

'He does it in Sainsbury's too,' I said. 'This is louder.'

We were bored after that so went back to the Silent Auction. Mummy was trying to be casual and avoid looking at the Lot 12 sheet.

'You're back already?' she asked.

'We had our turn on the fire engine,' I said.

'That . . . err, siren noise?' she asked.

'Yes?'

'Was that William D?'

'Yes,' I said.

'Thought so,' she replied, eyeing another mummy who

was getting uncomfortably close to the Lot 12 sheet. We held our breath, then let it out as the lady moved away. William D started whining about being bored. Mummy looked at her watch.

'There's only another few minutes before the Silent Auction finishes. I'm not abandoning my post now. We don't want a repeat of last year,' Mummy said, glaring at me.

William D slumped down dramatically on the floor and howled. Mummy rolled her eyes.

'Where's your father?' she asked me.

'In the beer tent,' I said.

'Could you please go and get him and ask him to take William D home?'

'I can't go into the beer tent,' I pointed out.

Mummy sighed. 'OK. I'll go and get him. You stay here and keep an eye on Lot 12. If someone else bids, then you outbid them, OK? I want that iPhone!'

'And to help the orphans,' I reminded her.

'Yes, yes, and help the orphans,' Mummy said absently as she headed off towards the beer tent.

So I hung around, watching the sheet for a while. Lots of people were now walking around the tables, inspecting the bids, some people were scribbling new bids on things. £12 for a meal for two at the Blue Anchor. £14 for a session at the ice rink. More people bid for Lot 6, the other iPhone.

Mummy was going to get her iPhone. I hugged myself

in excitement. Maybe she'd let me download some games on it.

'Just four minutes left to bid in the Silent Auction,' Mr Fowler's voice came over the loudspeaker. And suddenly a great influx of people rushed over, including Imogen and her mother. Oh no! I felt nervous. Imogen's mummy saw me and said hello. Imogen gave me her frenemy smile. Why can't grown-ups tell when other girls are being mean to you? It's the biggest thing in the world. It fills the room, this mean-ness, but parents just don't notice. Especially when it's their own daughter doing it.

'Have you bid on anything, Chloe?' Imogen's mummy asked me as she inspected the prizes and the bid sheets.

I hesitated, then said, 'Not much.' I tried not to look at Lot 12 but couldn't help my eyes from flicking over towards it. Imogen followed my gaze. Quick as a cat, she rushed over to the half-hidden Lot 12 sheet and looked at it. My heart sunk.

'Look, Mummy,' Imogen said, with a sly sideways glance at me. 'Hardly anyone's bid on this iPhone.'

'Waaaaahhhh!' screamed William D, louder than the siren on the fire engine.

'Gosh, that's cheap,' Imogen's mummy said. 'But you already have an iPhone, darling.'

I held my breath.

'Not for me, Mummy, for Casper,' Imogen said, smiling sweetly at me. Casper is Imogen's little brother, he's far too young to have an iPhone. It wasn't fair that he should have one when Mummy really wanted one but couldn't afford it. 'I'll buy it for him for his birthday. I'll use my own money.'

I peered over towards the beer tent but couldn't see Mummy.

'How thoughtful,' Imogen's mummy said. 'Now where's a pen?'

There was a pen on the table just next to me but they hadn't seen it yet. I lifted the table up a bit and it rolled off onto the floor.

'I have one in my bag,' Imogen said, pulling it out. Her mother took it and scribbled a number on the sheet.

'One minute to go in the Silent Auction,' Mr Fowler said.

I really like Mr Fowler, but just now I wished he'd shut up. I peered over towards the beer tent again. Still no sign of Mummy.

'I want Mummy,' William D yelled, still in a heap on the ground. People were stepping around him. There's always some screaming child slumped on the ground at events like this and it's usually William D. Imogen and her mummy moved on to look at some of the other lots. I scurried forward and saw Imogen had outbid Mummy by £1. The bid was now £71. Well, I wasn't going to let her get away with that. I ducked under the table and grabbed the pen I'd rolled onto the floor, then I stood and scribbled a new bid on Lot 12. £72.

But Imogen saw me. She scowled and came back. She wrote on the sheet: £73.

I glared right back at her. She wasn't going to push me around today, I decided. I wielded the pen again. £74.

'Thirty seconds to go in the Silent Auction,' Mr Fowler called cheerfully. 'Get your last bids in.'

Honestly, Mr Fowler, I thought. Give it a rest.

Imogen scribbled a number down on the sheet and turned back to me, triumphantly. I took my pen again and prepared to outbid her. But then I stopped. Imogen had outbid me by a long way. I looked up at her, shocked.

She smiled smugly. 'Daddy works for a bank, remember?'

I looked towards the beer tent. Finally Mummy had appeared and was sprinting back towards the silent auction. Daddy was trundling along behind her, more slowly.

'Ten seconds . . .' Mr Fowler called. 'Nine . . . eight . . . seven . . .'

'MUMMMYYYYYY!' William D screamed.

Mummy wasn't going to make it. Imogen was so confident she was going to win that she'd put her pen away.

'Five seconds . . . four . . . three . . .'

Time slowed down. Mummy held out her hand. William D screamed. Imogen smirked. She wasn't going to win this, I thought. No way.

I leaned down and wrote down one more number.

* * *

'One hundred and seventy-five pounds!?' Mummy shrieked.

'Sorry,' I said, even though I'd already said sorry quite a few times.

'The other iPhone only went for £148,' Mummy pointed out.

We were walking home. William D was still crying. Daisy was feeling sick because she'd eaten an entire bag of candyfloss. Mummy was cross with me for spending so much money. Only Daddy was in a good mood because he'd been drinking beer. He was walking a little behind us, singing a Katy Perry song.

'It's not even the new model,' Mummy went on.

'Sorry,' I said again. She didn't understand that I just had to beat Imogen. It wasn't fair that she was always so mean to me. It wasn't fair that her family had so much more money than ours. I wanted to explain this to Mummy but she wasn't really in the mood for discussing things like that.

'Anyway. It's for the orphans,' I said.

Mummy sighed. 'I know you were only trying to help, darling,' she said. 'But you can't go spending our money like that. You know things are tight.'

'I am a tiger, fighter, something inside her, cos I am a champion, come up and hear me roAAARRRR!' Daddy sang. He always gets the words wrong.

'I'm going to be sick,' Daisy said. And then she was, right in the middle of the pavement. Sausage, bread and cornflakes all pink from the candyfloss.

'Oh for heaven's sake!' Mummy snapped. 'Right, that's it! I've had enough. I can't do this any more.' She pointed a sharp finger at Daddy. 'You take over. I'm going home and going to my room for a lie down.' And with that she stormed off.

'Eeuugh!' Daddy said, looking at Daisy's sick.

William D stopped crying as we all gathered around to inspect it.

'Poor Mummy,' Daisy said. She looked a lot better after being sick.

'We need to do something to cheer her up,' I said.

'I know,' Daddy said. 'Let's all be on our best behaviour for a bit. Family Deal?'

'Family Deal,' Daisy and I chorused.

'I can see some sweetcorn,' William D said, pointing to the sick.

When we got home I decided it was best to stay out of Mummy's hair for a bit, so I went up to write some more of my report. The door to Mummy and Daddy's room was closed as I passed and I guessed Mummy was in there, having a lie down. I wondered what clever plan Daddy was going to come up with to cheer up Mummy. He can be pretty good like that sometimes.

Mummy and Daddy's Room

Mummy and Daddy's room isn't finished. Most of the house isn't finished, but Mummy and Daddy's room REALLY isn't finished. In fact it's not even started. There are big damp patches on the ceiling and some of the wallpaper is hanging off. Daddy found some old bits of carpet and put them on the floor but it doesn't look very neat and you always trip over the edges.

We're not officially allowed in Mummy and Daddy's room but that rule isn't strictly enforced. William D, for example, goes in two or three times a night, complaining about one thing or another and always wakes Mummy and Daddy up very early.

Mummy and Daddy have an en-suite bathroom. Their room looks out over the front of the house, like mine. Mummy would rather know what was going on in the street outside than look at the garden. She says there are two types of people in the world, street people and garden people. She's a street person and so am I.

Daddy is a little younger than Mummy. Next year

he's having a Big Birthday. Daisy thinks he's 50 but actually I know he's only 40.

Daddy likes reading. Like me. He's forever with his nose in a book, even in the middle of the chaos of our house. When the mood takes him he comes up with brilliant ideas for games. This is the man who invented BOOMball and Skink Hunt. Even Emily was impressed with Skink Hunt. Then there was the Sunday we woke up to find a note on the end of our beds saying:

FOLLOW THE STRING

And there was one end of a piece of string at the end of each of our beds, even Jacob's, and we all had to follow our length of string, winding it up as we went. We kept passing each other on the stairs saying 'good morning' and laughing. Except Jacob who said, 'This is stupid.' But he kept going anyway and I could tell he liked it. The string went upstairs and downstairs and out into the garden and around the shed and back through the rhododendron and around the side of the house and in through the front window until we all got to the end of our various strings and each found a present. I got a book I'd wanted, Daisy got a set of Moshi Monsters, William D got a Batman on a motorbike and Jacob got phone credit.

'Sweet,' Jacob said.

Part Four

Dark Cloud

The whole house is under a dark cloud. You know how in documentaries they sometimes show a mushroom cloud when an atomic bomb goes off? It's really dark and hangs overhead for ages. Well, our house is right underneath one of those at the moment.

Mummy is cross. It's not just that we disgraced ourselves again at the Summer Fair. She's still cross with me, for breaking the plate with William D's footprints on and also for feeding the bats. She's cross with Daisy, because Daisy used her make-up without asking and got lipstick on Mummy's favourite dress. She's cross with Jacob because he won't reply to her texts and keeps drinking all the juice and the milk and putting the empty cartons back in the fridge. She's cross at Clematis for bringing a live rat into the house then walking off, uninterested. She's cross at The Slug for eating a slug then sicking it up in the hall.

She's cross at Daddy for going to sleep in the shed instead of cutting back the rhododendron.

And this morning she found Sylvia on the shower curtain in the en-suite. There was a lot of shrieking. I felt bad for

Mummy, coming face to face with a snail in her shower, but I was glad that Sylvia was safe. I took her outside, said my goodbyes and released her into The Thicket.

Funnily enough, the only one of us not in trouble at the moment is William D, who hasn't brought home any notes this week. He's even got some stars on his chart.

It wasn't Sylvia who triggered the explosion today though. It was me. I can always tell when Mummy's going to flip. I can see it coming and am always very careful not to say anything that might push her over the edge. Daisy sees what I'm doing usually and joins in being nice to Mummy, or sometimes runs off to hide. But the boys? The boys are rubbish at telling what Mummy is thinking. Daddy just carries on as normal, William D seems to get worse.

Today we were having tea in the kitchen. Daisy, William D and I were sitting at the round wooden table, eating fish fingers. William D was squawking loudly and occasionally kicking me and Daisy.

'Ow!' we were saying. 'Stop it, William D.' Usually we'd complain to Mummy that William D was kicking us and she'd move him, or tell him off or something. But today I thought it was best not to involve her because she had a Face on.

Daddy was reading the 'Strange But True' bits of the newspaper out to Mummy and getting in her way as she moved around the kitchen, cleaning things up and trying to prepare our packed lunches for the next day at school.

I could see she was getting crosser and crosser.

'So apparently this man, Mr Awalayzi, woke up in the middle of the night,' Daddy was saying. 'He heard noises from the next room and grabbed his shotgun . . .'

'Mm,' Mummy said, tight-lipped.

William D kicked Daisy.

'Owww, William D!' said Daisy. Then, 'Mum . . .'

But I shook my head at her and she remembered we were trying not to make Mummy cross. I could see Mummy's earlobes were turning white; why does no one else notice things like that?

'. . . so he fires the gun and accidentally shoots his wife in the leg,' Daddy said as Mummy pushed past him to get to the fridge. 'When the police arrived he told them that he'd mistaken his wife for a wild pig.'

'Mm,' Mummy said again. Her cheeks were pale, with little spots of red. I held my breath. William D squawked like a parrot. He tried to get up from the table but I held him down and tried to give him some more food. Mummy's shoulders had gone all tight.

'According to the article, the man was released once the police had interviewed his wife,' Daddy went on. 'Mr Awalayzi is quoted as saying "I told them my wife resembled a pig and the police agreed with me, so I am a free man."' And with that Daddy nearly fell over laughing. Mummy had by now tightened up all the muscles in her body. She was clenched like a Pokémon ball. Usually at this point she explodes.

'That's funny, is it?' she asked.

'Yes,' Daddy said. 'Yes, it is.'

'So this poor woman has not only been shot by her husband, a man she thought she could TRUST. But she's now being mocked around the world because of her appearance? That amuses you?'

Daddy shrugged. 'Well, I thought it was funny,' he said quietly. I think finally he'd realised Mummy was cross.

We all waited for the explosion. There was complete silence in the kitchen, apart from the tick of the backwards clock and the hum of the fridge, which suddenly seemed very loud. Even William D had stopped squawking.

Mummy turned back to making the sandwiches. We all breathed a sigh of relief.

Then William D stood up again and picked up his plate. I tried to stop him and take the plate away from him but we got in a muddle and the plate slipped somehow and smashed on the floor and that was when Mummy exploded. She spun on her heels.

'That's IT! Go to your rooms!' she snapped at us. 'I need to talk to your father.'

'Can we watch telly inst—' William D began but Daisy sensibly bundled him out of the room and up the stairs. I followed but I stopped halfway up the stairs so I could listen to the row. I could see them both through the open door; Daddy leaning against the Aga, looking a bit pale, Mummy now flushed with colour.

168

'I can't do this any more,' she said. 'William D is driving me round the bend. He ran off again in Sainsbury's today. I panicked and rushed around looking for him. Some kind old lady found him for me and when I asked him to thank her he stuck out his tongue and called her poo-face. Where does he get this behaviour from?' she asked, staring at Daddy.

Daddy shrugged.

'And where the hell is Jacob? He's never home, he doesn't ring, he won't answer my texts.'

'Err,' Daddy said. 'I think I might have seen him on Monday . . .'

'You let them run wild, John,' she said. 'I can't do all the disciplining. I have four children to keep track of, I have a house to run and a job to do. I leave them with you to look after and they do nothing but make a mess.'

'I agree,' Daddy said, trying to say what he thought might calm Mummy down. 'I think the children could do more to help around the house.'

'Not just the children,' Mummy said. 'I've asked you a hundred times to cut that rhododendron. I can't get out of the house without ending up with beetles in my tights.'

'OK, I'll cut the rhododendron,' Daddy said.

'No you won't,' Mummy replied. 'You keep saying you will, but you won't. And you won't cut the grass, and you won't trim the hedges, and you won't fix the computer, and you won't replace the toner cartridge and you won't fix that wonky gate. You don't do anything I ask, but the thing you won't do the most is cut that . . . stupid rhododendron!'

There was a pause while Daddy stared at Mummy. She often got cross, but this was something else. She was bright red and her hair was all messy and she was wagging her finger at him.

'I'm sorry,' Daddy said, trying to hug her, but she pushed him away.

'I feel trapped,' Mummy said quietly. 'I'm stuck in a house with a door that doesn't work and a family that doesn't lift a finger to help.'

'You go and lie down,' Daddy said. 'I'll get the children bathed and into bed.'

'Yes, you will,' Mummy snapped, and she grabbed a magazine and stomped out of the kitchen and into the sitting room. I pushed myself against the wall so she wouldn't see me. 'And don't forget to do the washing-up,' she shouted back at him. 'And feed the cats!'

'OK, sweetie,' Daddy called after her. He came out of the kitchen, saw me and pulled an 'I'm-in-trouble' face. But I didn't laugh. Because he really was in trouble. We all were.

After the bath we wanted to go downstairs but Daddy said best to leave Mummy alone for a bit. So instead we played a game Daddy had made up called Murder in the Dark, which is like Hide and Seek but with all the lights off. I could tell Daddy had chosen this game because you have to be quiet and tiptoe around. One person is The Murderer and they have to stalk quietly around the house finding people and murdering them. The murdered person is allowed to scream one warning scream before lying down quietly. If you switch on a light you lose.

Poor old Daisy was completely terrified, of course, because of the ghost in the spare room. It was a brilliant game and everyone stayed very quiet and well away from Mummy. Unfortunately, we went on a bit late and eventually Mummy had to come and shout at us to go to bed but it was just normal, everyday shouting so I think Daddy had done quite well by letting her have some time on her own. Our hearts were racing after the game and we were so wound up we didn't get to sleep for ages. Daisy came into my room and crept into bed with me because she was scared of the ghost.

'Silly billy,' I said to her. But secretly I was glad she was there because what if there really was a ghost? Also I was a bit worried about Mummy. I hated it when she was sad.

Just as I was drifting off to sleep I heard Daddy out in the garden.

'DOOBY-DOOBY-DOO! DOOBY-DOOBY-DOO!'

Daddy

The next day was Monday. Mummy came in while we were having breakfast. William D had got up super early and woken everyone up. He was very grumpy and annoying. I think Daddy had gone back to bed after putting the telly on for him. William D hadn't wanted to come and eat any breakfast so we had to drag him. Daisy and I were exhausted. Mummy was in her business suit. She stopped when she saw us.

'Look at the bags under your eyes,' she said, shaking her head. 'This is what happens when you stay up all night playing games on a school night.' Then she looked over at last night's washing-up, which Daddy hadn't done. I jumped up and started doing it.

'Mummy, can I have –' began William D, but she held up a hand and interrupted him.

'I'm going in to the office early,' she said. 'If you need anything, ask your father. He'll take you into school today.'

'Bye, Mummy,' I said.

'Have a nice day at work, Mummy,' William D said. She kissed us and then was gone. Daisy and I shrugged and looked at each other. It was a quarter past eight. I think. It really is hard to tell with the backwards clock.

We finished our breakfast and Daisy and I did the rest of the washing-up while William D watched television. Daddy still wasn't up when we finished so we went and watched the telly as well while we waited.

AGES later he came to the door of the playroom and looked at us, puzzled. 'Why aren't you at school?' he asked. 'It's past nine.'

'You have to take us,' I said.

'Where's Mummy?' he asked.

'At work.'

'Uh-oh,' he said. He'd clearly forgotten he was in charge. 'Right, turn off the telly. Get your school uniforms on, now!'

'Excuse me!' William D roared as Daisy flicked off the telly. 'I'm the leader of this house!'

Ten minutes later we were in the car racing to school. Daisy had odd socks on, which she was not happy about. William D had his Ben 10 trainers on because we couldn't find his school shoes in time. I hadn't brushed my hair but it didn't look too bad. None of us had a packed lunch. Daddy said he'd drop something off later for us all.

'Why didn't you wake me up?' Daddy asked as we raced through a red light. William D had cheered up since Daddy started driving fast.

'Why didn't you set your alarm?' I asked. 'I thought you knew what you were doing.'

We screeched to a stop outside the school and we tumbled out. Daddy got William D out of his booster seat.

'Right,' he said. 'Off you go then.'

We all raced off into the school and I was about to go to my class when I suddenly remembered something. I stopped quickly. Daisy ran CRASH! into my back and William D ran SMACK! into hers.

'Hold on,' I said. 'Why's William D with us? He doesn't go to this school.'

So we all raced outside again and just managed to catch up with Daddy before he drove off.

'What's the problem now?' he asked, rolling his eyes.

'William D doesn't go to this school. You have to take him to St Andrew's.'

'Good point,' Daddy said. 'Come on, William D.'

'Awkward,' said William D.

'Why didn't you say something?' Daddy asked as he buckled William D back into his seat.

'I thought you knew what you were doing,' William D said.

'Well, I don't,' Daddy replied, climbing into the driver's seat. 'You need to help me out, OK? We all need to help each other out, OK?'

As we trotted back into our school we heard the screech of Daddy's tyres as he raced off towards town.

Sometimes I wonder if any grown-ups really know what they're doing.

I was tired later on at school. I just couldn't stop yawning. We had to work in groups in science and I was in a group with Tobias, Hannah and Imogen. Mrs Fuller often puts me in a group with Tobias because he needs someone who's good at helping but I don't know why she put Imogen in the group. We made a volcano out of clay and then we were supposed to mix vinegar and baking soda together to make it erupt. The smell of the vinegar made me think of Chip Shop Charlie and I was hoping Jacob would ask her out again and that she'd be coming over on Friday to collect him. The volcano wasn't erupting because Imogen had made the hole in the spout too narrow and it squashed together. I'd told her she was doing it wrong but she'd just ignored me. Imogen kept telling me it was my fault for mixing the vinegar and baking soda in the wrong quantities and she said I should let someone else have a go. She meant her, or Hannah, so I gave it to Tobias because he needs to be included but also to annoy Imogen.

Tobias hadn't really been paying attention so I explained he was supposed to mix the ingredients and shake them up. Before I could stop him he poured a sachet of baking soda into his MOUTH and then drank the vinegar.

Straight away the mixture started fizzing in his mouth and his eyes went all wide and he looked scared. Suddenly he spat white foam out all over Imogen, who screamed. Mrs Fuller came rushing over and took him to the sink to wash his mouth out as Hannah dabbed the furious Imogen down. I felt bad, not because of what happened to Imogen but because I obviously hadn't explained it to Tobias carefully enough. Everyone was laughing, but underneath the noise I heard Imogen mutter something to Hannah. I didn't hear it exactly, but I think she said something about Tobias. I think she used a word that isn't nice to use.

'What did you say?' I asked.

'Nothing,' she said.

'What did she say, Hannah?' I asked.

Hannah shook her head and didn't reply, but I could tell she didn't think it was OK, what Imogen had said. I think Mrs Fuller noticed something when she brought Tobias back and she asked if everything was all right.

'Everything's fine,' Imogen said. I just glared at her. Maybe I should have said something, but she would have just denied it. And I think she knew she'd got it wrong, using that word about Tobias.

Daisy and I went to Emily's after school and Daddy turned up a bit later with William D, who only had one shoe.

'Couldn't find it anywhere,' Daddy explained. 'Are

you sure you don't remember taking it off?' he asked William D.

William D shrugged and looked mystified.

That night, Mummy and Daddy had a long chat about things. I know because I sat on the steps and listened to them. I couldn't quite make out what they were saying but Mummy cried a bit and Daddy put his arm around her. I think they made everything better again because the next day, Mummy got us up, made breakfast and took us to school. I was pleased about the fact that she seemed happier, but the row had meant I hadn't been able to talk to her about the party. There's so much we need to do. Tidy the garden, clean the house, fix Front Door, organise food and games. Maybe it wasn't Mummy I needed to talk to, though.

Maybe Daddy was the key.

Jacob

Things were mostly back to normal the next day, which was a Tuesday. Mummy had stopped complaining about us and was instead complaining about Ellen Downing. Mummy had got a spiderweb in her face when she went through the rhododendron and had been still combing her fingers through her hair when we got to school. Imogen's mummy Ellen came over to 'help'.

'As one gets older, one needs to start thinking about cutting one's hair short, don't you think, Polly?' Ellen had said. And I could see Mummy's cheeks going red.

'Do you see how she looks me up and down?' Mummy asked Daddy after school.

Daddy stood leaning against the counter, with the cookery books behind him and the radio burbling in the background. Mummy was moving about, getting ketchup from the fridge for William D, or chopping up food for the meal she and Daddy were going to have later. They were having a glass of wine each. I was watching them carefully to make sure everything was going to be OK. I love these times, when we're all together in the kitchen, though usually William D ruins it by trying to get down before he's finished.

'She seems to think the school gate is actually a catwalk,' Mummy said. 'She stands there, with her Mulberry handbag, and her Alexander McQueen shoes and just judges everyone else.'

'Ellen? Is she the pretty one?' Daddy said.

'Do you think she's pretty?' Mummy asked, with thin lips.

'No,' Daddy said quickly. 'Definitely not.'

Mummy sent Daisy and me upstairs to see if Jacob was still alive. No one had seen him for days.

'Knock before you go in,' Mummy warned. 'You shouldn't sneak up on teenage boys.'

We climbed two flights to the second floor. I knocked and waited. No answer.

'Let me try,' Daisy said, knocking again. Still no answer.

I tried the door and to our surprise it opened. I don't know why, but I'd always assumed Jacob's door would be locked. The thought of going in there had never really occurred to me. The rest of us went into each other's rooms without thinking anything of it, but Jacob's room was different. It was a teenage boy's room, full of mysterious things and strange smells.

Daisy and I looked at each other, swallowed and went in.

It was just like I'd imagined. There were clothes all over the floor, a strong smell of deodorant and fungal foot powder and some type of manly perfume, but it couldn't mask the smell of Jacob's stinky trainers or his smelly underpants or the mouldy cheese sandwich on the windowsill.

'Poo-eey,' Daisy said, holding her nose.

'Well, he's definitely not in here,' I said.

Just then, we heard a buzzing noise.

'That's his phone,' Daisy said. 'He must have forgotten it.'

My *Nature Detective Handbook* says I should use my Observation Skills at all times. So I picked up the phone, to observe who was texting.

'It's Charlie!' I said, excitedly.

On Jacob's phone, when someone texts, you get the message appearing on the screen for a few seconds even when it's in sleep mode. If you want to look at it for longer, you have to put in the passcode, but for some reason Jacob wouldn't tell us his passcode. We knew Mummy's and Daddy's because they're the same and we watch them typing the numbers into their phones like thirty times a day. Daisy wrote their number on a Post-it so she wouldn't forget.

But Jacob was too clever for that. So I only got to see the text for a moment before the screen went black, but it said something like:

Hi you, great to see you last night. See you Friday? Cx

'Yay,' I squeaked, then did a fist pump. Jacob must have phoned her like he'd promised. They must have been on a date last night! We were going to see Charlie again.

I was about to tell Daisy what I'd just read, when we heard a noise from Jacob's little bathroom. A cough! He was here after all. Then we heard the toilet flush in there. Daisy let out a soundless shriek and we rushed from the room. Then I remembered I still had the phone. I stopped at the door, sprinted back to the bedside table and dropped it before racing out again, just as the bathroom door opened. Daisy and I rushed downstairs expecting Jacob to yell at us, but he mustn't have seen us. Inspired by my experience, I wrote about Jacob's room for the My House report.

Jacob's Room

I can't describe Jacob's room very well because none of us ever go in there. We sometimes get to peer around the door and see loads of clothes and shoes all over the floor, but that's about it. It's always dark because he never opens the blinds. Jacob has an en-suite bathroom. Daisy and I thought it was unfair that Jacob got a bedroom with an en-suite but Mummy said that Jacob should get it because no one else wanted to share a bathroom with him and when she put it like that we agreed.

Out of all of us, Jacob's room is the one we go into least, and he's the family member we see least of too. He hides himself away when he's at home and at other times he just stays away. He didn't used to be like this. When we lived in London he was always there and the door to his room was always open. Mummy says he's going through lots of changes. But I miss him.

I did go into Jacob's room today, as it happens, and can report that it is very smelly. There is jam on the floor and a pair of underpants hanging from the curtain rail. But it's odd because Jacob is always clean and smells lovely when he's not in his room. He's like a butterfly coming out of his manky old cocoon every day. In my house, just like in nature, appearances can be deceiving.

I got another surprise in Jacob's room today. I was really pleased to find out that my brother is going to go out with Charlie again. We all think he's made the right choice, we like her a lot. Sometimes it seems like Jacob's not very nice to the girls he goes out with but it looks like he's finally learned his lesson.

Rejection

When Mummy came to kiss me goodnight later, I asked her if anyone had responded to the party invitations. She paused before she answered.

'Emily has said yes,' she said. 'But I'm still waiting for a few others.'

She must have seen me looking disappointed because she hurriedly said, 'I'll make some phone calls tonight. I'll get it sorted, OK?'

'OK, Mummy,' I said.

What if no one comes to my party?

On the way home from school on Wednesday, we passed the fish and chip shop. Daisy grabbed my shoulder and stopped me. She pointed into the shop.

'What is it?' I asked.

'That's Charlie,' she said.

And it was. Her hair was tied back and stuffed into a horrible white hairnet, and she was wearing an awful yellow T-shirt that had the name of the shop printed on it: In Cod We Trust.

'Hi, Charlie!' Daisy yelled. Charlie looked up and waved us in.

'Hello!' she said.

'Are you going out with Jacob on Friday?' Daisy said.

Charlie blinked in surprise. 'Don't beat around the bush, will you? I'm afraid Jacob hasn't asked me if I want to go out with him on Friday.'

'Why not?' I asked. I didn't understand it. We'd seen the text she'd sent to Jacob two days ago. She wanted to go out with him again. He must have responded. He'd promised me.

'I don't know,' Charlie replied. 'Maybe he had a better offer.'

'But we like you!' Daisy said.

'Aww, that's so sweet,' Charlie said. 'I like you guys too, but it was just a couple of dates. Sometimes they lead to more, sometimes they don't.'

'Do you like Jacob?' Daisy asked. I shushed her because it was such a personal question but Charlie answered anyway.

'I do like Jacob, he's funny and sweet. But I think maybe he has some issues?'

'You mean his feet?' Daisy asked.

'I mean he can't seem to decide who to go out with. He's seeing someone new every week.'

Then Charlie had a customer and it was time to go. She waved and smiled as we left.

'She recognised us,' Daisy said, excitedly.

'She's so lovely,' I said. 'Even in that hat. Why won't Jacob just choose her?'

When we got home I asked Mummy about the invitations again and she put her hand on my shoulder and told me she'd called around but loads of people had said they couldn't make it on that day.

'But we can have your party anyway,' Mummy said. 'It'll just be smaller.'

'No one will come,' I said. 'Everyone is going to be away.'

'This is why Ellen got in first and moved Imogen's party to the Saturday BEFORE school breaks up,' Mummy said.

'I think we should cancel,' I said. 'I'd just rather go ice skating with Emily and Daisy and Tamsin maybe?'

'Are you sure?' Mummy asked. She looked sad for me. 'Maybe we could arrange another thing later in the summer, when your friends are back?'

'OK, maybe,' I said.

When she'd gone I lay in my bed. Imogen had spoiled things, just like I knew she would. I suppose I could have gone ahead anyway, but there wouldn't be many people, and we still had to sort out the garden, and Front Door and the flappy wallpaper and Mummy was so stressed I didn't feel I should ask her to try to sort this out too. It was easier just to go ice skating, that way I didn't have to be worried about who to invite and who might turn up, or not turn up.

This way, I wouldn't be disappointed again.

Quiet Dad

That night I set my alarm for four a.m. then went downstairs with my duvet and waited in the sitting room until I heard Cara's milk float humming down the road. I climbed out of the window. It was a bit chilly but I had my Ugg boots and my dressing gown on so it was OK.

'Hi, Cara,' I said.

'Hey. If it isn't my little assistant,' Cara said. 'Your parents know you're here?'

'Oh yes,' I lied.

'Well, climb aboard,' she said. 'Fancy a gossip?'

'Yes please,' I said.

'You tell me your news first,' she said as we set off. 'Then I'll fill you in on mine.'

'Um, well, Daddy still hasn't mowed the lawn. But William D is getting loads of stars on his star chart. He hasn't brought home any School Lunch Reports for a while. Or Accident Reports. Mummy says it's because he's on the School Council now and has learned responsibility.'

I had to stop chatting then for a bit because Cara

had stopped the float and it was time to make some deliveries.

I'd done this a few times now, so I knew what everyone had. Two pints for Mr Rogers at number 41, one pint and an orange juice for the Guptils at number 47. My conversations with Cara had lots of breaks in them as one or the other of us would go off to leave a delivery by someone's front door. Cara doing the even numbers, me doing the odds.

'How are things with that Imogen?' she asked.

I filled her in on the Birthday Wars. She snorted when she heard about Imogen's manoeuvring.

'You know what it is, yeah?' she said. 'She's afraid of you.'

'No, she isn't,' I said.

'Yeah, she is, she thinks you're more popular than her and prettier and cleverer and all that. That's why she has to fight dirty.'

'I don't want to fight at all,' I said.

'That's because you are a good person,' Cara said.

I wasn't sure that Cara was quite right about Imogen being scared of me, but it was nice to hear her say it.

'So pick a new date, and you go ahead and have your party,' Cara said.

'I've told Mummy I don't want one at all,' I said.

'Tell her you've changed your mind,' Cara said firmly. 'After all, you don't turn eleven every day.'

'Hmm,' I said.

After that I told her about Charlie and how we weren't sure if Jacob was ever going to ask her out again.

'She's the one,' I insisted.

'Ah, you can't tell people who they should be with,' Cara said.

'Even if it's totally obvious?' I asked.

'It won't be obvious to him,' she said. 'Trust me. You have to let him make his own mistakes.'

I sighed and got out of the cab. It was my turn to take the order, this time to the Dukes' house.

'Only one orange juice,' Cara said as I picked up a bottle.

'But they have two a day, except Sundays,' I said. I'd known this even before I started helping Cara. I could always see it in the morning as Shouty Dad would come out in his slippers and say, 'I'M GETTING THEM NOW! YOU DON'T HAVE TO GO ON ABOUT IT!'

'HE always wanted two orange juices,' Cara said. 'But he's moved out.'

'He what?'

'They had a big row,' Cara said. 'He moved out on Friday.'

Come to think of it, the street had been quieter the last few days. Apart from us playing BOOMball and screaming 'DOOBY-DOOBY-DOO!' at the cats, of course.

'So he's gone?' I asked, dismayed.

'He has,' Cara replied. 'I saw him leave myself. Packed

up his car and drove off, just as I was finishing my round.'

'Maybe he's just gone to visit his mother,' I suggested after coming back from Mrs Simpson's house where I'd dropped off a solitary milk bottle. There was a light on in the upstairs window and I wondered if Mr Simpson was inside, reading there. Jacob says that she probably murdered him like she did her other two husbands. I know he's joking. At least I think he's joking. I hope Mr Simpson is OK.

'His mother lives in Eastbourne,' I added. 'I know because he shouted it out one time: "I'M GOING TO VISIT MY MOTHER IN EASTBOURNE!"'

'Shhh!' Cara said, laughing. 'Look, darling. No man takes three suitcases if he's going to visit his mother.'

'Oh,' I said.

'Or a beer fridge,' Cara added. 'He's moved out, all right.'

I was sad. Not just because I wasn't going to get to watch Mr Duke shouting at his family on a lazy Saturday morning any more. It was more than that. I don't like change. I like our house, and our street, and I want things to always be like this.

Also, if Mr Duke can move out like that, it means other people can move out.

People like Mummy.

Retreat

When I got into the house I could smell toast, which could mean only one thing. Jacob was home. I went into the kitchen and he jumped a mile when he saw me. Why was everyone so shocked to see me today? Had I grown horns or something?

As Jacob made me toast, I asked him when he was going to see Charlie again. He shook his head and looked worried.

'I don't think it's going to work out with me and Charlie.'

'What?!' I said, outraged. 'She's lovely. Nicer than Bella.'

He shrugged. 'What can I say? I guess she just didn't like me very much.'

I nodded. 'Yes, that must be it,' I said.

'Hey,' he replied, looking hurt. 'Why is that the likeliest reason?'

'You shouldn't give up so easily,' I said. 'You have to work hard to fulfil your dreams. This is just the start of your journey.'

'You've been watching the *X-Factor* again,' he said, pointing a bit of toast at me.

'Promise me you'll call her and ask her out?' I said.

'I promise,' he said.

It was still very early and I went back to my bedroom after that and sat on the window seat looking out at the world, worrying about Shouty Dad. I didn't hear Mummy calling me for breakfast. She had to come up.

'Time to get up,' she said, looking a bit pale. 'Put on your uniform and come down for breakfast.'

First I had to go for a wee and when I came downstairs it turned out I'd forgotten to put my uniform on and Mummy's cheeks went red. William D wasn't helping her mood. He was having a meltdown because we'd run out of his favourite breakfast cereal.

'I'm sorry!' Mummy said to him, sharply. 'I'm sorry I had to cook and clean and take you to school and work and pick you up from school and take you to football and take the girls to ballet and bring you all home and cook and clean all over again. I'm sorry this meant I was a little rushed in the fifteen minutes I had to do the shopping and I'm sorry I forgot your stupid Captain Haribo Sugar Rings.'

I could see it wasn't the right time to tell Mummy I'd changed my mind about the party again. I'd just have to wait. Then Mummy found that Jacob had finished the orange juice AND the milk and put both the empty cartons back in the fridge again.

'Right!' she snapped. 'That's it. House meeting. Right

here. Right now. Go and find your father, Chloe. Bring Jacob too.'

I rushed upstairs and found Daddy in his en-suite listening to the radio and singing into the hairdryer. When he saw my face I think he realised he'd better get downstairs sharpish. Jacob, though, wasn't in his room. Daddy texted him and we discovered he was working early shifts at the garage. We were all a bit nervous because we hadn't really done anything about all the things Mummy had been cross about last week. I kept breaking plates, Daisy had spilled perfume on Mummy's favourite cardigan, William D was . . . well, William D was William D. And Daddy? Daddy hadn't done anything in the garden, and he'd made the computer worse – you couldn't switch it on at all now.

'Can I see the agenda for this meeting?' Daddy asked.

'No,' said Mummy. 'I was going to leave this until tonight but maybe you need to hear it now. Since no one in this house pays any attention to me and since no one in this house does their jobs, even after being asked a thousand times, I've decided if I can't beat you, I'm going to join you. I'm not going to do anything either. For a whole week.'

'What, not even the cooking?' I said. The truth was, though Daddy was excellent at making spaghetti carbonara and OK-ish at spaghetti Bolognese, he couldn't actually cook anything else. Much as I liked spaghetti, I didn't want it every day for a week.

'I won't be doing the cooking, the cleaning, bathtime, cat feeding or bed-making,' Mummy said. 'And to make sure I don't give in to temptation, I'm not even going to be here.'

We all stared at her in astonishment.

'Where will you be?' Daddy asked.

'I'm going on a retreat,' Mummy said. 'I've been thinking about this for a while now. And I'm just going to do it. In the first week of the school holidays I've arranged time off work. I'm going to a little place in the woods and I'm going to learn meditation and eat raw foods and re-charge my yin. And my yang.'

'Who's going to look after us?' William D asked.

'Your father is going to look after you,' Mummy said. 'He's going to cook, and clean, and wash, and iron . . .'

'Err, hang on,' Daddy said.

'. . . and do bathtime and storytime and bedtime and feed the cats and apologise to Mr Coleman when he comes around to complain about something and all the other thousand jobs I do around here.'

'Will you pop back to visit us?' I asked, worried.

'No visits, no phone calls, no texts, no internet,' Mummy said. She must have seen my face because she held my hand. 'It's only for a week, it'll be good for us all.'

'But what about my work?' Daddy said.

'That's your problem,' Mummy said. 'Work from home, take a holiday, call in sick.'

There was silence around the table as we took this in. We all looked at Mummy, who seemed deadly serious; we all looked at Daddy, who swallowed nervously.

Then Mummy stood up, picked up her tea, and said, 'I'm going to miss you all terribly, but the more I think about this the more I'm sure it's the right thing to do. You all need to step up. Not being here is the only way to force you lot into action. I'm throwing you all in at the deep end. Meeting adjourned.'

It looked as though I wouldn't get my party after all.

Part Five

Taffeta

The doorbell rang. It was Friday, so that could only mean one thing! Daisy and I looked at each other, grinning.

'Charlie!' we cried.

'He must have texted her after all!' I said. Together we rushed to Front Door. We even got there before William D for once, but he just charged past us and lifted the letterbox.

'Hey, Sexy Lady,' he yelled. 'Woop-woop Gangnam-style.'

'Hello?' we heard from outside.

'Shush, William D,' I said. Daisy and I yanked at Front Door but she wouldn't open. Daisy pushed William D out of the way.

'It's stuck again,' she shouted through the letterbox. 'Go through the window.'

I rushed into the sitting room, slid the window up and stuck my head out.

'Hi, Charlie,' I said, cheerily, but then my mouth dropped. It wasn't Charlie. It was another girl. A blonde girl with too much make-up and a very, very short skirt. Her hair looked all big and a bit tangled, to be honest. It looked like it could do with a brush.

'Who's Charlie?' she asked.

'Sorry,' I said, embarrassed. 'Why are you here?'

She blinked and looked annoyed. 'I'm here for my date with Jacob.'

My mouth dropped. How could this be? Who was this girl? What about Charlie? We'd all really liked her and didn't want some new girl coming along and elbowing her off the sofa.

Still, maybe I should give her a chance.

'The door's stuck,' I said. 'You can come in through the window, or go around the back.'

This was the real test, of course.

'I'll just wait for Jacob,' she said, coldly.

I was a bit surprised by this. No one had ever said that before.

'He'll be ages,' I said. 'He always is. Come in and you can drink some water.'

'Gosh, thanks,' she said, not looking impressed. 'I'll go around the back.'

'There's a rhododendron,' I said. 'You might get twigs in your hair but Jacob doesn't mind things like that.'

'I've just had this done,' she said, pointing to her hair and rolling her eyes.

'Really?' I said, surprised. 'Probably best to come in through the window, then. We have a mirror and I can get you a brush if you like.'

The girl tutted and came over to climb in. Well, she made a right dog's breakfast of climbing through, I can tell you. William D shook his head. Daisy put her face on and I tried to help by pulling the girl's skirt down just in case Daddy walked in. But it was Mummy who came in, not Daddy.

'Hello,' she said to the girl. 'Which one are you, then?'

'I'm Tabitha?' she said, as though Mummy should have known.

'Hello, Tabitha, I'm Jacob's mum. Sorry about the door being stuck. It is such a pain having to come through that rhododendron, isn't it?'

'I came through the window,' Tabitha said, sniffing.

'Oh,' Mummy said, looking at Tabitha's mad hair. 'It's just that . . . I thought . . .' She tailed off.

'Can I get you a drink?' I asked.

'No thanks,' Tabitha said, not even looking at me.

I elbowed Daisy and nodded. I've been trying to encourage her to talk more in these situations. Daisy looked at her notebook where she had written some pre-prepared questions.

'Do you have any transferable skills?' she asked.

'What?' Tabitha replied. 'Will Jacob be long?'

'I'll get him,' William D yelled, rushing for the stairs.

'No, I will! I will! You went last time,' Daisy shouted, rushing after William D and trying to pull him back. They fought their way up the stairs, making a terrific clattering.

Mummy, Tabitha and I stood for a moment looking at each other awkwardly. Then Mummy said, 'Right, well, I'll leave you in Chloe's capable hands. Don't keep Jacob out too long, will you? Ha ha.'

'Bye,' Tabitha said, as Mummy left.

'Are you at the college?' I asked her.

'Yes,' she said. I waited for her to say something else. But she didn't speak again, she just looked around at the pictures and books on the shelves.

'Do you have a job?' I asked.

'No,' she said.

This was hard work. I didn't think Tabitha was going to get to Boot Camp, let alone Judges' Houses. In the silence that followed, we could hear William D and Daisy shouting over each other to tell Jacob the news that Tabitha was here.

'There's a girl here . . .'

'. . . her name is Taffeta . . .'

'. . . and she has black knickers on.'

'She's quite rude . . .'

'. . . and she has really messy hair . . .'

I smiled awkwardly at Tabitha. She didn't smile back and it seemed ages before Jacob finally came down. This time Front Door wouldn't open even for him. I don't think the door liked Tabitha any more than the rest of us did. Tabitha had to go through the window again, though now Jacob was here she'd started smiling and giggling and pretending she thought it was fun.

She didn't say goodbye. Once they'd gone, we all looked at each other. I shook my head.

'It's a no from me, I'm afraid,' said William D.

'Maybe she was just shy,' Daisy said. Daisy always sees the best in people, but I could tell she didn't really think it in this case.

'I want Charlie back,' I said.

'Me too,' Daisy said.

'Me three,' William D added.

'AGH!' said Mummy from the kitchen. 'John! Stop sneaking up on me!'

That night it started raining hard and was still going the next morning. I woke up and listened to the thrum of the drops against my window. This was the Saturday when I was originally going to have my party. The fact it was raining made me feel a little better about not having my party that day. It would have been rubbish if we couldn't go outside. But I was also a bit disappointed because Emily was supposed to be coming over to play BOOMball.

Over breakfast Mummy got a phone call.

'Hello, Ellen,' she said, sounding surprised. Imogen's mummy never calls. 'No, darling, I'm really sorry but we don't have a marquee.'

Suddenly I remembered that it was the day of Imogen's party. Mummy made a funny face at me and I giggled.

'I know, *darling*,' Mummy said. She didn't usually call people 'darling' unless she was being sarcastic. 'It's terrible bad luck. We've had such lovely weather and on the day of the party, too. Yes, yes. No, I'm sure the weather in Barbados will be so much better.'

After she put the phone down she turned to me, mouth open. 'The nerve of her, phoning to see if we have a marquee when you haven't even been invited to Imogen's party!'

It's wrong to feel happy when someone else's party is spoiled but I couldn't help myself.

Daddy came downstairs hobbling and groaning.

'What's wrong, Daddy?' I asked.

'I've done my back in,' Daddy said.

'It's my fault,' Mummy said, looking sheepish. 'I might have accidentally given him a little fright.'

'On purpose!' Daddy said.

'Accidentally on purpose,' Mummy confirmed. 'Well . . . you're always doing it to me.'

'I don't do it on purpose,' Daddy protested. 'She hid in the cupboard,' he explained to me. 'And when I came out of the bathroom she leaped out at me, shrieking "DOOBY-DOOBY-DOO!!"'

'I couldn't think of anything else,' Mummy said, trying not to grin.

'So I slipped over in surprise and hurt my back,' Daddy said.

I giggled.

'I'm sorry, John,' Mummy said. 'I forgot you're nearly forty. Your reactions aren't what they used to be.'

'It's not age related,' Daddy said, lowering himself

gingerly into a chair. 'It's being terrified-by-your-wife related.'

It was good to see them back to normal. If anything that happens in this house can be described as 'normal'.

Anyway, because Daddy's back was sore, and because it was raining, and because Mummy was going away in a week, we decided to have a quiet, family weekend at home. Jacob was nowhere to be seen, which was annoying because I wanted to ask him what had happened to Charlie. I worked on my project and we played Crime Scene Investigations and Mummy took William D to the toyshop to buy him a Pokémon because he hasn't brought home any School Lunch Reports for ages, or Accident ones for that matter.

On Sunday the weather was a little better. Daisy and I took some cushions down to the summerhouse and turned it into the headquarters of the Deal Detective Agency. That was brilliant because it stopped me worrying for a bit about my birthday and Shouty Dad and Mummy going away.

But I didn't sleep very well on Sunday night because the worries came back.

Happy Birthday

The last week of school went really quickly. On the Monday I handed my report in; it was the last piece of coursework to be completed. Mrs Fuller said she was really looking forward to reading it. As I was leaving for lunch, I stopped and went to see her.

'Hi, Chloe,' she said. 'Is everything OK?'

'Yes. It's just . . . about my report.'

'What about it?'

'Do you think I could have a copy of it? There's someone I'd like to show it to.'

Mrs Fuller smiled, nodded, and after lunch she dropped a big envelope on my desk with a crisply photocopied sheaf of papers inside.

After that we just messed about for the last couple of days and I managed to stay clear of Imogen. I think I might have shouted at her if I'd seen her.

We celebrated my birthday on the first Saturday of the holidays. When I woke up there were loads of presents at the foot of my bed, just like Christmas. I think Mummy must have been waiting for me to wake up because soon after everyone came rushing in and gave me big hugs and

William D helped me open my presents, by which I mean he opened my presents for me but I didn't mind. We had pancakes for breakfast, my favourite. Later on we went ice skating. I liked the skating but overall things were a bit up and down. I didn't want to use the penguin that helps you stand up and so I fell over about fifty times and bruised my bottom. So that was a down. William D had been left at Granny Jean's for the day because Mummy was terrified of what he might get up to on an ice rink. It was so busy there it was a very good idea. He would have gone berserk. So William D not being there was an up. We played a great game where we went around doing a conga and then we did ice line-dancing, which was hilarious. We had a break for smoothies and Emily laughed so hard at something blue smoothie came out of her nose and that was the uppest bit of all.

Everything was going really well until Tamsin tried to jump over a traffic cone, fell over and sprained her wrist. That was definitely a down. Maybe, in hindsight, bringing Tamsin ice skating wasn't the best idea. When she hurt her arm, she went all white and stopped smiling for a bit and said 'What am I like?' very quietly. So we all had to go to the hospital. Some of the nurses knew Tamsin's name. We sat in the A & E waiting room for ages and we all took turns playing on Mummy and Daddy's phones until they ran out of batteries. That was another down bit.

The nurses put Tamsin's arm in a splint and she was

much better after that and we all went to Pizza Express and did make-your-own pizza and the grown-ups came and drank wine down one end of the table and we stayed AGES and it was really good fun and definitely an up bit. But underneath it all I was worried about Mummy and her retreat. I could hear the grown-ups talking about it.

'It sounds WONDERFUL,' Vicky Bellamy said. 'Just what you need.'

'I'd love the chance to escape too,' Tamsin's mummy said.

'We all would,' Tamsin's daddy said.

Our daddy didn't say anything, but he looked a bit worried. Mummy was leaving tomorrow. That was definitely a down.

I forgot all about it, though, when Jacob turned up. He was really funny and sat with us rather than with the grown-ups, which I thought was really nice of him. He gave me a new book in hardback that he'd bought with his own money and I gave him a big hug. I like having an older brother. That was a really big up bit.

Over all, it was a good birthday. But a party would have been better. I should have listened to Cara and got Mummy to rearrange the party for later. You don't turn eleven every year, after all.

It was just then that I started to have a bit of an idea.

Sunday

'DON'T GO!' William D screamed. He was clinging to Mummy's leg and being dragged along the pavement.

'Oh, sweetie, it's just for a few days,' Mummy said. She was being all brisk and business-like. She bent down to pick him up, but he wouldn't let go. I was trying not to make a fuss myself. I could see Mummy was really upset too and I didn't want to make it worse for her. I tried to remember what Daddy had said. That this was important for Mummy to do. She needed some time on her own and we needed some time without her to learn how the washing machine worked.

Daddy plucked William D off Mummy's leg, still howling, and squeezed him tight. Mr Coleman stuck his head out of his front window and scowled at us. It was quite early in the morning. Usually we don't wake him up for another hour or so.

Mummy gave Daisy and me a big hug. She whispered in my ear, 'I love you.' Then she kissed Daddy, who said: 'Don't worry about a thing.'

'I'll worry every second,' she said. Then she almost

ran into the car and drove off. I think she might have been crying but she didn't show her face.

Daddy had organised lots of activities that day to keep us busy. We went to the park with Emily and Tamsin, and their mummies. We played rounders, which was fun except for when William D got the ball and ran off with it. Even if he was supposed to be batting he'd just drop the bat and catch the ball instead then run off with it.

After that we went back home with them all and played Skink Hunt, which you can only play in the back garden because of the long grass. The Skink needs to be able to hide. But then Daisy got bitten by some creature and while Daddy was looking for something to put on it Tamsin climbed up the apple tree and got stuck because of her sprained wrist. So she had to be rescued and it was all very funny.

Later on we took blankets and cushions down to the back of the garden and pushed our way through The Thicket to get to the summerhouse. Tamsin climbed on the roof again but didn't fall over the fence this time.

'It's our secret clubhouse,' Emily said. 'We can hide here from your silly daddy.'

'He's not silly,' I said. Sometimes Emily can be a bit rude.

'He never tidies, he hardly ever goes to work, he can only cook one thing, spaghetti carbonara,' Emily said.

I was about to tell her to be quiet when Daisy got in first.

'He's not silly!' Daisy snapped. She stood up and clenched her fists while we all looked at her in surprise. Daisy doesn't get cross very often. 'He's funny and clever and actually works very hard!' She paused for a moment, glaring at Emily before adding, 'And I LIKE spaghetti carbonara.'

Emily was quiet after that. I think she knew she'd been the silly one to be rude about our dad. I was a bit surprised that Daisy had said all that. She usually won't say boo to a goose so I was proud of her for standing up for Daddy. But all this talk about daddies got me thinking about Mummy, and her retreat. I was feeling sad but then I started to think more about my idea of how to fix everything. The Big Plan. I was wondering whether to mention it to Emily and Daisy when Tamsin fell over the fence again and we had to rescue her without Mr Coleman spotting us. What with all the fuss I decided not to tell the others about the Big Plan. I haven't really thought it all through yet anyway. Emily and Tamsin stayed for dinner and Daddy sang Emily Bellamy to the tune of 'Let it Go' from *Frozen*.

Emily. Bellamy-y-y
You're always coming round for tea-e-e
Emily. Bellamy-y-y
You love my spa-ghetti
I don't have

Any gar-lic bread.
Don't moan at me . . .
It's not very good for you anyway.

As usual, Emily just stared at him, but it doesn't put Daddy off.

As it turned out we'd run out of spaghetti as well as garlic bread so Daddy made us Experimental Pizza with Bolognese sauce on it. It was a bit strange, especially with the big lumps of carrot, but we were all so hungry we demolished it. Emily went home after that and Daisy gave her a hug to show everything was OK. Daddy let us stay up to watch a DVD while he snoozed on the sofa. We chatted most of the way through the film.

'I was worried you were going to say something mean to Emily about her daddy before,' I said to Daisy.

'I wanted to,' Daisy said. 'But that wouldn't have been nice.'

'I was very proud of you,' I said.

'She shouldn't have said those things about Daddy,' she said. We looked over at him, snoring on the sofa with his feet on the coffee table. Mummy doesn't let him do that when she's around. Daisy snuggled up to Daddy and poked him to stop him snoring. Then she went to sleep and I stayed up watching DVDs until Jacob came home and made us all go to bed.

So, overall, it was a good day.

But it would have been better with Mummy there.

Monday

It was the first day of the holidays that wasn't a weekend, which is when the holidays properly start, I think. As usual I woke first and went to sit on the window seat. It was a cloudy day and there were spots of rain on the glass. No one passed in the street below. Things were quiet without Shouty Dad. I heard William D get up soon after and go into Daddy's room and start whining about going down to watch telly. I don't think Daddy had had much sleep because he got cross very quickly.

'Fine, fine,' he said, storming downstairs to turn on the telly. Soon after I heard the sounds of Pokémon from the playroom and coffee smells from the kitchen came floating up the stairs. I sat there for ages, just looking out at the world before I suddenly realised I was going to have to go down and sort out my own breakfast. I missed Mummy calling up to me to come down. I thought of her being very relaxed and happy at the retreat and that made me feel a bit better. I dragged Daisy out of bed as well and we padded down in our nighties.

'OK, people,' Daddy said at breakfast. 'I'm a bit stuck

today. There's no way around it, I have to go into the office in London for a couple of hours.'

'Who's going to look after us?' I asked. 'Can we go to Emily's?'

'No, they're visiting Emily's grandparents today. I've tried calling loads of people but everyone's away.'

'What about Jacob?' Daisy asked.

'He's not answering his phone,' Daddy said.

'Did you text him and ask if he could look after us?' I asked.

'Yes, why?'

'Schoolboy error,' I explained. 'He always "loses" his phone when you ask him for a favour.'

'Ah. I'm learning so much already,' Daddy said solemnly.

'So what are you going to do?' I asked.

'Only one thing I can do,' he said. 'I'm taking you all to London.'

'YESSSSS!' William D yelled, standing up on his chair and raising his fists.

It took quite a while to get everyone organised to go. Every time it seemed we were ready to leave, Daddy would notice something wasn't quite right. We were out on the pavement by the time we realised William D didn't have any shoes on.

'You can't go to London without shoes,' Daddy said. 'Chapter One of the Parenting Handbook.'

Then it was everyone needing a cardigan, then a

raincoat. Then I pointed out that we had nothing to do on the train so we had to go and get colouring things and books. Then we had to go back and leave some food for the cats. We very nearly missed the train.

The train was PACKED. We don't often go to London, but when we do we go on the weekends and there's hardly anyone on. We sometimes get a carriage to ourselves, especially if William D is feeling energetic. But today it seemed like everyone in Weyford had decided to take this train. There were no seats, which William D was outraged about. We had to stand all the way. Lots of people were talking on their phones very loudly about work things and others were tapping the screens on their devices. One lady had a stack of spreadsheets and was flicking through them, staring at little tiny numbers. I shuddered. No one was talking to anyone else.

'Tell Karen to wait till I get there!' a large man with a red face shouted into his phone. 'Do NOT let her talk to the client.'

'Excuse me,' William D said, tugging on his trouser leg. 'You're really winding me up.'

But the man didn't seem to notice. I tried to read my book, but there wasn't much room and my legs got tired and William D started whining before we even got to the next station. Daisy and I looked at each other.

'I don't want to be a commuter when I grow up,' she said.

'Me neither,' I agreed.

Eventually we got to Waterloo and that was a bit scary. It was much busier than it is on the weekends. Pigeons flew overhead and a man with a suitcase on wheels nearly knocked me over. Daisy and William D clung to Daddy's hands and he only has two so I had to walk behind them. Daddy took us down to the Underground, which was even more crowded and grimy and noisy.

William D loved the tube train ride but even he looked a bit scared as it went around a corner and the lights went out. As the shrieking wheels ground against the iron rails sparks lit the carriage with a ghostly flash. When we got off we had to wait for ages for a lift to take us up to street level. Everyone was very tall and grumpy. Daddy led us slowly down the pavement, past black cabs and red buses and cyclists doing mad things, until eventually we got to his office.

We'd taken quite a long time to get there so Daddy had to rush into a meeting and he left us with a man called Nick who was the receptionist. He had a nose ring and a tattoo. William D pulled on my sleeve and pointed to him.

'Awkward,' he whispered very loudly.

'Shush, William D,' I replied.

'What does a receptionist do?' Daisy asked Nick.

'I make people cups of tea and then I look at Facebook,' Nick said.

Nick made us hot chocolate and let us go on the computer. Then we played Swivel Chair Rodeo, where you spin someone on the swivel chair until they fly off and crash into something. Daddy came out of the meeting after a while and went to get us sandwiches from Pret, which we ate in another meeting room. People in IT have lots of meetings. Nick came and ate with us and I asked him lots of questions.

'Do you like working in IT?' I asked.

'No,' he said. 'I hate computers.'

'Except Facebook,' I said.

'Except Facebook,' he agreed.

'I don't think Daddy really likes computers either,' I said.

'To be honest, Chloe,' he said, leaning towards me, 'I don't think anyone here really likes computers. It's just a job.'

Poor Daddy, I thought, having to come up on the train and work in a job he didn't like. Eventually it was time to go. We said goodbye to Nick who I think had quite enjoyed having us there.

'Makes a break from looking at Facebook all day,' he said and Daddy laughed because Daddy thought he was joking. Nick winked at me to show that he wasn't. Sometimes the best way to sneak the truth past someone is to pretend that it's a joke.

On the way home we got to Waterloo early and got seats on the train. We sat near the loos and the seats we

217

had were the ones that flip up when you're not sitting on them. I think some of the grown-ups who got on afterwards were a bit annoyed that their seats had been taken by children but we were all EXHAUSTED and didn't care. William D had a difficult journey. He kept standing up to look at something, then he'd forget his seat had flipped up and would sit down again and crash to the floor. It was only funny the first time. I had to take him to the loo twice and we forgot to press the button that locks the door so someone else came along and opened the door and it slid back slowly to reveal William D standing on the toilet seat doing a wee.

'EXCUSE ME,' he shouted and we all laughed. But after that he started to get tired and whiny and hungry and Daddy couldn't calm him down and he fell back into someone's lap and spilled their coffee and it wasn't much fun, really.

'I really want to get off this train now,' William D complained.

'Everyone wants you to get off the train,' the man he'd spilled coffee on said.

I think Jacob must have been home because the kitchen was all tidy when we got back. Not for long, though. Daddy cooked Experimental Pizza AGAIN, which meant getting a margarita base and adding random things from the fridge to it then smothering it all with cheese. We were all starving so it tasted really good, apart from the pickled onions, but that's the great thing about

Experimental Pizza, you can just pick off the bits you don't like. Daddy let us watch TV after that because we were all so shattered.

'Do you know what?' he said. 'I think we might just be able to do this.'

'Do we have to go up to London again?' I asked.

'No,' he said. 'I won't have to go in again until next week now. I do have to do some work at home tomorrow, but I was wondering about us taking a little fun trip on Wednesday.'

'Alton Towers?' I asked. 'The swimming pool?'

'Err, no,' Daddy said. 'I just meant to Home 'n Garden Megastore.'

'Oh,' I said.

'Sorry, I hope you're not too disappointed?' he said. 'I thought we could get some tools to help us in the garden.'

'I'm not disappointed at all,' I replied. 'In fact, I've been hoping we could go to the garden centre.'

He didn't look like he believed me, but I was serious. This all fitted in very well with my Big Plan.

That night I dreamt Mummy came and gave me a long cuddle and a kiss.

'I miss you,' Dream Mummy said.

'I miss you too,' I replied.

Tuesday

There were some stains on the table. Big purple stains. None of us were quite sure what had caused them or who had done it. William D was looking a bit guilty, but he often does so that's no guide.

'Where does Mummy keep the cleaning things?' Daddy asked, looking under the sink.

'In the cupboard under the stairs,' I said.

Daddy and I went to look for something to clean the stains off. There were lots of bottles in there.

'Bleach, window cleaner, toilet cleaner, glass cleaner, wax, polish, wood cleaner, disinfectant,' Daddy read as he picked up bottle after bottle. 'So this is where all the money goes.'

'Mummy likes to have the right cleaner for every surface,' I explained.

'I think it might be OCD,' Daddy said.

'No, she buys it from Costco,' I said.

The stains didn't come off, even with Oak Wood Table Cleaner, new and improved formula.

'Maybe it's not oak,' Daddy suggested. 'Is there any Teak Wood Cleaner?'

But there wasn't, so Daddy decided we'd bring our trip to Home 'n Garden Megastore forward to today. 'After all, we haven't been there for ages,' he said.

At the store Daddy told us to keep an eye on William D while he went to look at wood cleaners.

'Don't let him near the lift,' Daddy said. Last time William D got stuck in there for twenty minutes.

We went straight to the paint section and I chose 'Hushed Riverbed' and Daisy got more lilac.

'Hi Chloe,' someone said. It was Hannah.

'Hi,' I said. 'I thought you were on holiday.'

'We only went camping for the weekend,' she said. 'Mummy and Daddy are decorating this week.'

Her parents were talking to a bored-looking shop assistant about fancy paints. Hannah rolled her eyes at them. She looked even more bored than the shop assistant.

'Oh,' I said. 'Imogen said everyone was on holiday, so that's why they had to have her party so early.'

'I'm not on holiday. And neither is Sophie.'

I swallowed. 'Would you . . . If I had a party? Not this Saturday, but next Saturday, would you come?'

'Definitely,' she said. 'And Sophie, I bet. If she's invited?'

I nodded and couldn't help myself grinning. The Big Plan was coming together nicely.

'Where's William D?' Daddy said, suddenly arriving. I looked around frantically, but he'd gone.

'He's so sneaky,' I said.

'Sneaky as a doorknob,' Daisy said. 'Where could he be?'

'The lift!' Daddy cried, and we all ran like crazy.

When we got to the lift we heard a thin whining noise, similar to the one you hear in Sainsbury's when William D hits the big red button. A man in a HGM shirt was peering up through the glass door at the lift, which seemed to be stuck between the floors.

'Press the button and hold it down,' he yelled, but there was no answer. 'Hold on,' the man called. 'I'll go and get the key for the emergency override.' He disappeared.

Daddy stepped forward.

'William D?' he called. 'Can you hear me?' But again there was no answer. We were starting to really worry by the time the man came back. He plugged a key into a panel at the side of the lift and turned it. The lift started coming down, very slowly. It's one of those special lifts for disabled access that is just a sort of platform with rails and no roof.

'I told you to keep an eye on him,' Daddy said to me.

'I did, but . . .'

The lift hit the bottom and the HGM man pulled the door open.

The lift was empty.

'What? How? Where?' Daddy said, his mouth hanging open. The man with the key looked surprised too.

'How did it get to where it was without someone pressing the button?' the man said.

Then we heard a shout from the upstairs bit where they display all the furniture.

'Yeah, baby!' William D yelled, jumping on a bed. 'I'm back in the game!'

Operation Napalm

Apparently when the lift stopped between floors William D had climbed up on the handrail and, because there's no roof on the lift, he somehow managed to clamber up and over the door, where a nice lady had helped him down. She'd asked where his mummy was and he'd run off. He is SO naughty! Daddy was so cross that he didn't buy any sweets for any of us so Daisy and I got cross and we all shouted at each other in the car and went to our rooms when we got home. All Daddy bought was a new spade and a saw for cutting branches. I didn't really think that was going to be enough to sort out The Thicket but I didn't say anything. What a disastrous trip.

Later on, though, Daddy said sorry and that he shouldn't have left us in charge of William D and also he was sorry for shouting at us, and he gave us some sweets he'd found in the cupboard which were fine even though they were a year over their best-before date.

After lunch we all put on our gardening clothes and went outside to get started on the new gardening plan. Or Operation Napalm, as Daddy called it. Daddy said we should all change into something we didn't mind getting messy. This was a necessary first step in the Big Plan. We assembled in the long grass just outside the back door and looked out at the jungle. The grass was up to my waist and up to Daisy's armpits.

Daddy was wearing a pair of bright red overalls that we'd never seen before. William D was wearing some old pyjamas.

'Do you really want to wear those?' Daisy asked. 'You're supposed to wear something you don't mind if it gets torn or muddy.'

'I hate them,' William D said. 'I want them to get torn AND muddy.'

Daisy was wearing the clothes she used to paint her walls lilac with tester pots. An old pair of trackie bums and a sweatshirt that used to be mine. Whenever I grew out of something it was offered to Daisy before being taken down to the charity shop. She was always very polite about refusing and would say that it was because she thought the orphans needed my torn jeans with the oil stains more than she did. But she had taken the sweatshirt because she knew it had been my favourite and she didn't want to offend. At first I'd worried she'd get paint all over it but Daisy's very neat and it still looked smart. I was wearing my Bri-Tech T-shirt and a pair of jeans that are starting to get a little tight for me. I also had wellies and a pair of tough gardening gloves. We were ready. It was time for the first part of my Big Plan to be put into action.

William D took a few steps forward into the grass and was immediately lost from sight. The bushes were all overgrown and choking each other. Brambles twisted around branches of trees and nettles had swamped the flowerbeds by the fence. A single red rose stretched up, out of the tangle, striving for sunlight like a rainforest tree.

We couldn't even see into garden two.

Daddy looked down at his feet.

'Didn't we used to have a patio?' he asked. 'I'm sure there was a patio here when they showed us around the house. Maybe they took it with them when they moved.'

Daisy was on her knees, pulling up grass. 'No, it's still here,' she said. 'Just covered with grass.'

'Right, well, that's the first job,' Daddy said. 'We'll reclaim the patio. No point venturing too far out into the garden on the first day.'

'Mummy said she wanted us to do the rhododendron first,' I said.

'Mummy has many excellent qualities,' Daddy said. 'But she is not a gardener. The outside is my domain.'

'OK,' I said, doubtfully. I looked over at Mummy's veggie patch, the only well tended part of the garden, but I didn't say anything because I didn't want to puncture Daddy's enthusiasm.

'It'll take us, what, half an hour to clear the patio?' Daddy said. 'Then we'll work our way around the side, clearing everything as we go until we get to the rhododendron. Another half an hour for that and we'll stop for supper. Maybe we could eat outside on our new patio!'

'Yes, please,' Daisy said.

I wasn't convinced Daddy was being realistic about the schedule.

'I'm sure there's a wooden picnic table somewhere,' Daddy said. 'Maybe in the shed.' He swished his way through the long grass in the direction of the shed.

'Daddy!' I called. 'Shouldn't we do the patio first, before we look for the table?'

'You get started,' Daddy shouted without turning around. 'I'll be back in a flash.'

Daisy and I looked at each other and shrugged. I picked up my trowel and hunched down. It was hard to scrape the grass out of the cracks between the paving stones. I gave up on the trowel after a bit and started trying to pull the grass up, but it was properly rooted under the stones and just too thick. Daisy was plucking individual blades of grass.

'I think you need to pull out the roots,' I said.

'How?' she asked.

'I don't know.'

'We need Daddy,' she said. We looked up but couldn't see Daddy coming back.

Then it started raining so we went back inside.

We didn't get much more done in the garden, except Daddy found the picnic table. The main problem, apart

227

from the rain, was the table was under lots of other things in the shed, and Daddy decided he needed to sort out the shed first and he sort of got involved and didn't do much else. Daisy and I cleared a few paving stones after the rain stopped, but then a shadow fell across me and I looked up. William D was standing there, with a huge grin on his face, absolutely covered in mud. His pyjamas were torn to shreds and as he turned around to give us a complete view I saw he had a squashed slug stuck to his back.

'What have you been doing, William D?' Daisy asked, horrified.

He shrugged. 'Gardening.'

By the time we'd got him inside and had cleaned up all the mud he brought into the house it had started raining again. I stood at the open kitchen door, looking out at the rain falling on the tall grass and the overgrown shrubbery. Normally I like the smell of the garden when it rains but not today.

I felt bad about not doing as much as I'd hoped.

Good Talk

That night, Daddy let me stay up a bit later than the others. We both liked to watch *Real Homicide Detectives* and Daddy thought Daisy was too young for it. She didn't mind as it meant she could go up to her room and practise her ballet in front of the mirror. She doesn't really practise much, she just pouts at herself and changes clothes and puts on make-up she's 'borrowed' from Mummy's room.

'So,' Daddy said after a while. 'How are . . . things?'

'What sort of things?' I replied.

'You know. School. Friends and all that.'

Daddy didn't usually ask about that sort of thing. It's not that he doesn't care. Just that his head is in the clouds.

'Did Mummy tell you to ask me?'

'Yes,' he admitted. 'But I do want to know.'

I shrugged. 'Sometimes I really like school. But sometimes . . .'

And then it all came flooding out. About how horrible Imogen was, and how she made me feel. How she was spoiling school for me and I didn't know what to do.

'Oh, Chloe, I'm so sorry to hear it. You haven't spoken to your mother about this?' he asked gently.

I shook my head.

'I don't want her to worry about me,' I said. 'She has enough worries already.'

Daddy shuffled over and put his arm around me. He smelled of pizza and aftershave and I snuggled into him and shut my eyes.

'You can talk to Mummy or me about anything, any time,' he said. And the sound of his deep voice vibrated against my chest. 'Would you like me to call the school tomorrow and talk to them?'

'No,' I said.

'Why, because you're worried you'll be called a snitch?'

'No, because it's the holidays and the school is closed.'

'Oh yeah,' he said, laughing.

'And maybe things will be different in Year Six,' I said.

'They will be,' he rumbled. 'We'll make sure of it. Things will be better.'

Then I wanted to change the subject.

'Daddy, is being a lawyer a transferable skill?'

'Yes, very much so. You can do law . . . stuff anywhere in the world, in theory.'

'Thanks,' I said, though it hadn't been the answer I was hoping for. I followed up with another question, wanting to keep him talking so I wouldn't have to go to bed. 'Do you like your job?' I asked.

He paused before answering.

'What makes you ask that?' he replied.

'Yesterday, at your work, you looked really tired and sad when you came out of the first meeting and had to go into the second one. Also, Nick said no one really liked working there.'

'Nick said that?'

'Yep.'

He looked at me seriously. 'Hey, I don't want you to worry about work. Maybe sometimes Mummy and I moan about it, but grown-up jobs are often full of exciting challenges and I'm sure you'll find the right one for you. It won't always be easy but you'll find it satisfying, believe me.'

'I'm not worried about what it'll be like when I start work,' I said, although a little bit of me did think that. 'I'm worried about you.'

He looked at me for a long time and then gave me the biggest hug.

'Don't worry about me, Chloe,' he said. 'I'm fine.'

'But don't you feel like you want to escape sometimes?' I asked when the hug was finally over.

He laughed. 'Sometimes, maybe. But only from the job, not from you lot.'

So why did Mummy want to escape? I thought.

Wednesday

'So things aren't going well?' Cara asked the next morning, as the milk float hummed down York Road. I don't know why I'd woken so early, but maybe Dream Chloe decided she needed to speak to Cara.

'No,' I said. 'There are no clean clothes, we're all sick of Experimental Pizza. Daisy's run out of knickers. None of us are sleeping well, especially William D. Daddy thinks that if he lets him stay up till late that means he'll sleep in longer in the mornings.'

'Does that not work?'

'No, the opposite,' I said. 'Mummy says it's like training for a marathon. You don't train for a marathon by never doing any exercise. You've got to practise sleeping and build it up.'

'So he gets up early? He might make a good milkman,' she said.

I think Cara likes it when I help her. I don't really think she finishes her rounds any quicker. I do tend to drop bottles from time to time, and we have to stop and clean up the broken glass. And then there are all the chats, which slow her down. But she hasn't told me to stop yet.

'Have you heard from your mother?' Cara asked after dropping off Mrs Simpson's order.

'No,' I said. 'She's turned off her phone and her email. I really miss her.'

'She misses you too,' Cara said. She stopped the float and trotted off down the path to Mr Thoreau's front door to plonk down his grapefruit juice.

'So why did she go?' I asked when she'd returned. 'If she misses us, she should come back, or at least phone.'

'She needs a break,' Cara said. 'Sometimes you just need to cut yourself off and escape. I went to a retreat once.'

'Really?'

'Yes, I just had to get away from it all. No float, no work, no milk.' She put the float into gear and we hummed off up the quiet street. Dawn was breaking and the blackbirds were starting to sing.

'Did you like it?'

'Hmm,' Cara said. 'Not sure. I missed having milk in my tea. It was all herbal infusions.'

'Did you sleep in?' I asked.

'I tried. But I'm a creature of habit. I found I'd get up early and couldn't find anything to do. So I started delivering sachets of herbal tea to all the other rooms. There wasn't anything else to deliver, you see, but I had to deliver something. It's in my blood. You can't change who you are, Chloe. Your mummy will be back soon and you'll remember just how much she loves you all.'

'Really?' I asked.

Cara stopped the float and turned to me with a big smile. 'I'm sure of it. Being a mummy is in her blood, you see. Now, get moving, it's your turn. Two pints of semi-skimmed for the Guptils.'

As Cara dropped me off outside our house, she grabbed my arm and handed me a big box of eggs. 'Take these, I'll put them down as breakages.'

'Thanks,' I said. 'Hey, Cara, would you like to come to a party?'

'I love parties, as long as they don't go on late.'

'This will be a daytime party,' I said.

'I'm there,' Cara said with a grin.

When I got into the house I counted them and she'd given us twenty-four eggs. That's a lot of eggs to get through. Especially as William D hates omelettes. But it was kind of her.

I went back upstairs and tried to sleep, but I just lay there thinking about what Cara had said. She'd seemed very sure, but what if she was wrong? Last night I'd asked Daddy if being a lawyer was a transferable skill and he'd said it was. Mummy could go anywhere and be a lawyer, just like Cara could go anywhere and be a milk-lady.

What if being a lawyer is in her blood, more than being a mummy?

Stakeout

'There is DEFINITELY a ghost in the house,' Daisy said to me at breakfast.

'This again?' I sighed. 'There are no such things as ghosts.'

'So how come you never go into the spare room?' she asked.

'There's no need for me to go in there!' I said.

'You're scared.'

'I'm not having this argument again,' I said.

'You know yesterday how I'd run out of knickers?' she continued.

'Yes.'

'Well, this morning, my drawers had been filled up with clean clothes, including all my knickers.'

'Daddy must have done it,' I said.

Daisy looked at me like I was crazy.

'Or Jacob,' I suggested.

'Be serious, Chloe,' Daisy said, rolling her eyes.

'Do you really think it's more likely that a ghost did it?' I asked.

She shrugged and I shook my head.

'Also, I got up to go to the loo in the night,' she said. 'And I heard something in the spare room. It sounded like a ghostly rattle of chains. Or possibly someone snoring.'

'Did you go in to see?' I asked. The skin on the back of my neck was prickling. Daisy shook her head. Later when I asked Daddy if he'd done the washing, he said that he hadn't.

'In fact,' he said. 'I was hoping you could help me find the washing machine.'

So if it wasn't Daddy it must have been Jacob . . . Mustn't it?

After breakfast Daddy needed to get on with his 'work' so sent us out into the garden to find the mower but we forgot and played Skink Hunt all morning instead. At one point I looked back towards the house and thought I saw a curtain twitch in the spare room. Maybe Daddy had gone up. Or maybe Daisy was right and there was a ghost in there.

At lunch I talked to Daddy about the Big Plan. It was time to get the others involved.

'A party?' he said. 'But you had the thing at the ice rink.'

'It's not just a party for me,' I said. 'It's a party for all of us. For Mummy and you and Jacob and Daisy and William D, and all our friends from the street.'

Daddy looked at me for a bit, then he smiled. 'That's a fantastic idea,' he said. 'I love it.'

'I want to have it in the garden,' I said. 'So we'll need to cut the grass and clear it all up.'

'Err . . .' Daddy said.

'If we all work together we can get it done, can't we?' I said.

He nodded. 'Definitely,' he said. 'Now, let's eat.' He opened the fridge and blinked in surprise.

'Where did this food come from?' Daddy said. I was sure he meant the eggs, and he did, but there was lots of other food there too that had just appeared. Daisy gave me a knowing look and mouthed the word 'GHOST'.

'I don't know,' I said. 'Did Jacob buy it?'

Daddy snorted. 'There's lettuce and cucumber. Jacob wouldn't buy salad. He hasn't eaten anything green since he swallowed that Play-doh in Reception class.'

'We should do a stakeout,' Daisy whispered to me. 'Tonight. We'll catch the ghost.'

'There isn't a ghost,' I said.

'Then where did the food come from?' she hissed. 'How did my knickers get washed?'

I rubbed my chin. She had a point.

Emily and Tamsin came over that afternoon to play and when they found out about the stakeout they asked if they could stay over. Daddy shrugged his shoulders.

'Sure, two more, three more, why not invite the whole street?'

Because of the food that the ghost had brought, we

had a proper meal that night: chicken stir-fry followed by Mini Magnums. After dinner Daddy took a huge pile of spreadsheets into the sitting room and went to sleep on the sofa while we watched about a hundred DVDs. He eventually woke up and told us all to go upstairs. After we'd got William D into bed, we pretended to go to bed ourselves but instead we all sat around in Daisy's room in the dark, telling ghost stories until we heard Daddy's bedroom door close downstairs. I popped my head out into the hall. All the lights in the house were off except the little night light on the second floor landing, which is there so that Daisy can find the loo in the dark.

And so the stakeout began. We each had a torch. At first we thought we'd go on regular patrols around the house, but all the ghost stories we'd been telling had got us terrified by that point and none of us wanted to go anywhere. Instead we all snuggled under the duvets. Daisy and Tamsin were on Daisy's bed. Emily and I were on the spare bed. The door was half open, so we would be able to hear the groans of the ghost as it passed, and see its ghostly glow. It was a windy night outside and the house seemed especially creaky. We chatted for a while, but then I think we might have dozed off because the next thing I knew Emily was shaking me and saying.

'It's the ghost! It's coming up the stairs!'

'You saw it?'

'I went to the loo, and I heard something downstairs,'

she replied excitedly. 'I looked over the banister and there was a figure coming up. Dressed like a monk.'

'A monk?'

'With a cowl, you know?'

I sat bolt upright, my heart pounding. Emily fumbled for her torch but I pushed her hand away.

'Don't,' I said. 'It'll realise we're here . . .'

Bravely, I got out of bed and stepped slowly towards the door. Daisy and Tamsin were snoring in the other bed. I reached the door and turned around to look at Emily. I nearly jumped out of my skin when she loomed up RIGHT behind me. I hadn't heard her following.

'You're coming too?' I asked.

'I still need the loo,' she explained.

Emily was right, something was coming up the stairs, slowly, and accompanied by a ghostly glow. I waited until the ghost was right outside the door and made sure I had my finger on the button of the torch. Then quickly I flung the door wide open and shone my light at the hooded figure outside.

'Aaargh!' said the ghost, leaping back.

'Aaargh!' said Emily and I, leaping back.

'Aaargh!' said Daisy and Tamsin, woken up by all the screaming.

The cowled figure lurched into the room, making Emily, Tamsin and Daisy scream again. But I didn't scream because by that stage I'd realised it wasn't a ghost at all. It was . . .

'Jacob?'

'Chloe, what are you doing up so late?' he asked. 'You scared the bejeebers out of me.'

'Emily thought you were a ghost,' I said, glaring at her. I realised now that his cowl was just his Gap hoodie. The ghostly glow was the light from his phone screen.

'Can I go to the loo now?' Emily said. 'I'm desperate!'

It turned out Jacob had been on a date.

'With Charlie?' Daisy asked hopefully.

'No,' he said. 'With Tabitha.'

'Boo!' Daisy said.

'How did it go?' I asked.

'Not great,' he said.

'Yay!' said Daisy. Which I think was a little unkind.

He offered to make us all a midnight feast and we trooped downstairs trying to be quiet but actually making the house orchestra play its creaky tune. Jacob made us all toast with jam and told us about his date. Nothing had been right for Tabitha. She didn't like the film, then they went for a burger and the chips were too cold, then they'd gone to a party at a friend's house and she'd had a row with another girl and ended up crying on the stairs.

'I had to walk her home, all the way over on Friary Street,' he said. 'I didn't even get a kiss.'

'Was Charlie at the party?' I asked.

Jacob looked at me with one raised eyebrow. 'She was, as it happens,' he said.

'We like Charlie,' Daisy said.

'I know you do,' he said.

'Why don't you ask her out again?' I said.

Jacob looked guilty for a bit. I'd got him. Then he sighed. 'I really like Charlie. She's pretty and funny and clever.'

'So why don't you want to see her again?' I asked.

'You're going to think it sounds silly, but . . .' He paused and took a mouthful of toast.

'But what?'

'I hate the smell of vinegar,' he said finally.

'What?'

'I hate the smell of vinegar,' he repeated. 'She smells of vinegar all the time. It's like dating a gherkin.'

'That's the only reason?' I asked.

'I told you it would seem silly,' Jacob said. 'But every time I'm with her, I can smell vinegar. I kissed her once and I could smell her perfume, which I liked, but then underneath it, in the background, there was this smell of vinegar.'

'That doesn't sound like a good reason not to go out with someone,' Daisy said.

Emily snorted. 'Men,' she said.

'All right, don't gang up on me,' Jacob said. 'I know it's a rubbish reason, but that's how I feel.'

There was a pause in the conversation after that. Jacob looked uncomfortable. He hates confrontation. Emily was giving him evils. I was disappointed in him. I thought the leopard had changed his spots.

'Where's your mummy?' Tamsin suddenly asked me.

'Have you only just noticed she's not here?' Daisy said. 'She's on a retreat.'

'I miss her,' I said. 'I don't see why she needs to stay there for so long. She could come back and visit us.'

'Well, she's also trying to make a point,' Jacob said. 'She just wants us all to appreciate how much she does for us.'

'I already did,' I replied softly.

Thursday

Emily and Tamsin stayed all day. We played in the garden a bit. Emily can sometimes be a little bossy when we play games and if she doesn't get her way she can get really grumpy. Daisy got cross with her for trying to change the Laws of Skink Hunt. Daisy hardly ever gets cross but NO ONE is allowed to change the Laws of Skink Hunt except Daddy. To distract them from the row I tried to get everyone to help do some weeding but then it started raining, and everyone was tired from staying up so late and waking up early, and we didn't get much done.

We came inside and argued about what to watch on the telly for an hour or so.

'OK,' said Daddy, coming in. 'Who's staying for dinner? It's Experimental Pizza tonight.'

We groaned. 'Not again.'

'Well, what else do you want? The magic food is all gone. There's salad?'

'No thanks,' I said. 'What about fish and chips?'

'Excellent idea,' Daddy said. 'I'll write a list of everything we need and you can go and collect.'

It wasn't just because I fancied eating fish and chips that I'd suggested it. I wanted to see Charlie again. I was hoping she'd be part of the Big Plan. There was a long episode where Daddy tried to find a pen. Eventually he made a spreadsheet of all the things we had to buy and printed it off. Then Tamsin got her hair tangled up in some coat hangers in Daisy's cupboard and Daddy had to chop some of it off. I think he was regretting saying Tamsin could stay for dinner. While he was caught up in hair and coat hangers, he sent me and Daisy to get the fish and chips. It was only us two because Emily was in the middle of a game of Top Trumps with William D.

We felt very grown-up as we walked down the street to the chip shop, carrying a twenty-pound note. Mummy probably wouldn't have let us go by ourselves, even though it was still light. We talked about how far we could get if we just jumped on a train with the twenty-pound note. In Cod We Trust is in the middle of a row of shops near the train station. It's a bit grubby around there. As we approached I saw a pigeon pecking at a squashed chip. I like all animals, but some more than others, and pigeons are definitely others.

'Hi, Charlie,' we said as we went in. We were the only customers.

'Hi, girls,' Charlie said. She leaned over the counter to look at us. There was a strong smell of vinegar in the shop. Daisy and I looked at each other knowingly. We gave Charlie our order and she wrote it on a slip of paper and stuck it on a spike so the cook could start frying.

'Have you been enjoying your holidays so far?' she asked.

'Yes,' I said. 'But Mummy has gone on a retreat and we miss her a lot.'

'I wish I could go on a retreat,' Charlie said. 'Somewhere they don't deep-fry everything.'

'Are you going to go on another date with Jacob?' Daisy asked.

'I think that ship has sailed,' Charlie said. 'Sorry.'

She gave us extra chips and threw in the mushy peas for free. Just before I left, I turned and said, 'Charlie, if I had a party, would you come?'

She nodded and smiled. 'I'd love to, yes.'

'I really like the smell of vinegar,' I said.

'Err, me too,' Charlie replied.

'Some people don't, though,' I said. I tapped the side of my nose, which means you are being subtle.

Charlie looked a bit puzzled.

'Some people really like chips,' I went on. 'They really, really like chips. But they just don't like the smell of vinegar.'

Charlie nodded and smiled.

'She means Jacob,' Daisy said. I looked at her furiously but she ignored me and tapped her nose. 'He doesn't like the smell of vinegar.'

'O-OK,' Charlie said, slowly. 'I think I understand.' She tapped her nose solemnly.

The fish and chips smelled delicious and the paper parcels were almost too hot to hold as we walked back. I don't like to have vinegar on my chips but I like the smell of it on Daddy's. It's a nice smell. Clean and honest and sharp. Just like Charlie. Jacob was silly.

Everyone was starving by the time we got back and we all fell on the food, the golden batter of the fish all crisp around the edges and a little softer in the middle. We picked out the little, crispy chips first because they were cooler and ate those, all salty and oily, then pulled off big chunks of fish with our fingers and blew on the soft white insides to cool it down. Daddy shared his mushy peas with us and I decided next time I was going to order those too, but Daisy and Tamsin didn't like them. William D kept eating the chips when they were too hot and then he'd stand there, mouth open, eyes wide, pointing into his mouth.

We had to explain to Daddy what he had to do next. What Mummy does for him. She actually blows on the food when it's in his mouth. It looks funny, blowing into a little boy's mouth. But it's either that or he spits the hot food out over the table.

After dinner Tamsin's parents came to pick her up. They were really pleased that she wasn't injured, even though her hair was uneven after the coat-hanger incident. I walked Emily back over the road to her house.

She stopped before she went in and turned to me.

'I like your dad,' she said.

I waited for more but that was all she said. That was enough, though. It meant a lot coming from Emily. I felt bad for her that she didn't have a nice daddy like ours. I gave her a hug, which she put up with for about half a second. She's not very huggy, Emily.

Daisy and I did the washing-up when I got back. There isn't much washing-up with fish and chips so we think we got a pretty good deal. As I stood there, drying the knives, I looked out into the back garden at the little bit of work we'd done and all the work we hadn't done. Tomorrow would have to be the day. The last day before Mummy came back. The day when it had to happen. My Big Plan.

So after dinner, just before I went up to bed I went out again into the garden in my pyjamas and wellies. There was something I just had to do.

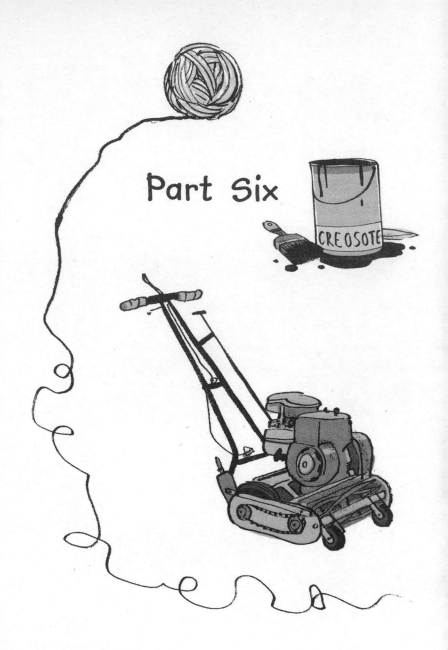

Part Six

The Summerhouse

I got everyone up early for breakfast on Friday. I don't know how to make scrambled eggs or bacon. But I'm good at toast. I got out orange juice, all the cereal boxes, milk, sugar and put the kettle on for Daddy. Then I went and woke everyone up, except Jacob, who didn't even answer when I bashed on his door. Daisy was hard to get out of bed too. I shook her, and tickled her, and poured a bit of water on her face. All she did was mutter and curl up under the duvet. But I kept at it and eventually managed to get them around the breakfast table, yawning.

'Straight after breakfast,' I said, 'we're going to start work.'

'On what?' Daddy asked.

'On the garden,' I said. 'You're going to mow the lawn before you do anything else.'

'I've told you,' he said. 'I can't find the mower.'

'So what's that?' I asked, pointing out of the French doors. Everyone got up to look. In the middle of the patio, looking a little worse for wear, was the mower.

'Where did you find that?' Daddy asked. He looked mostly pleased.

'I did a girl look, instead of a boy look,' I said. 'It was under the big apple tree, behind a holly bush.'

'Well done, Chloe,' Daddy said. 'What are you going to do, while I'm mowing?'

'We'll be working on the summerhouse,' I said. 'Cleaning the windows, sweeping the leaves. Chopping the brambles back. Can I use the loppers and the shears?'

'Will you cut off any of William D's fingers?' Daddy asked.

'No,' I said.

'Then yes, you can,' Daddy confirmed.

But after breakfast everyone sort of drifted off. Daddy went to check his emails. William D went to watch telly and Daisy headed upstairs.

'Where are you going? I asked.

'I'm going to get changed,' she said.

'You don't need to get changed,' I said. 'William D, turn off the telly. Daddy, turn off the computer.'

Everyone protested but I stamped my foot on the floor.

'Listen!' I snapped. 'Mummy will be back tomorrow. We have one last day to try and get this house looking welcoming. I want to show her how much we need her. I want her to think this house isn't something she wants to escape from, but somewhere she wants to retreat to. And I NEED YOUR HELP.'

They all stared at me, looking surprised.

'Who's with me?' I asked. There was a pause, then someone said:

'I'm with you, Chloe.'

We turned around and looked to where the voice was coming from. At the kitchen doorway stood Jacob. He smiled and winked.

'What do you need me to do?' he said.

So it began. All five of us working together in the garden. It was a cloudy day and I was a little worried it might rain, but it held off for the morning, at least. Firstly Jacob and Daddy looked together at the grass.

'We're going to need a strimmer as well as the mower,' Jacob said. 'It's just too long.'

'Leave this to me,' Daddy said. He moved a chair over to the fence, stood on it and peered over.

'Morning Mr Coleman,' he said.

'Morning,' I heard Mr Coleman reply.

'You'll be glad to hear,' Daddy said brightly, 'that we've finally decided to do something about all the weeds in our garden.'

'I am glad to hear that,' I heard Mr Coleman say. 'How am I expected to eradicate weeds and wildflowers on my lawn when all manner of spores and seeds are floating over from your side?'

'Well exactly,' Daddy said. 'The purity of your lawn is very important to us. So that's why we need to borrow your strimmer.'

Well, Mr Coleman could hardly say no after that. So he passed the strimmer over the fence and Daddy began cutting back the grass on our lawns. It took Jacob quite a while to get the mower going but once he did it ate up the grass Daddy had shortened, growling and roaring like a monster. Clematis and The Slug hid inside from the noise. Daddy sent me across the road to borrow some more gardening tools from Vicky, who has a lovely garden. Vicky and Emily came back with me, carrying hoes and rakes and loppers.

Later on Tamsin came over too and straight away walked through a stand of nettles and had to be dabbed with calamine lotion.

I was glad we had so many people helping, because it took ages to cut back all the vegetation around the summerhouse. You had to cut it, then pick it up and put it in a garden bag. Tamsin and Daisy were very naughty and threw some bits over the fence into Mr Coleman's garden and he popped his head over the fence and shouted at them. Jacob started a bonfire to burn up the cut-off bits, but that was too slow so Daddy started making trips to the dump. The hardest was the massive old rhododendron around the summerhouse. Daddy and Jacob sweated and gasped as they sawed off some big branches and dragged them away to the bonfire. But as soon as they'd done that, the summerhouse was transformed. It wasn't gloomy inside any more. It looked bigger, and brighter. It had been kept mostly dry under the shelter of the trees so it was in great condition but Daddy found a couple of holes where the damp had got in. He went and got something from the shed, a tin full of black, sticky liquid.

'Creosote,' he said. 'For sealing roofs.'

He climbed up a stepladder and painted the roof of the summerhouse; it didn't smell very nice but when he'd finished it looked really smart.

Jacob found the barbecue hidden in the long grass, and for lunch cooked sausages for us all on it. We had them in soft white rolls with loads of butter and brown sauce. We'd all been working so hard we were ravenous and I don't think I've ever tasted anything so good. While we were eating lunch, the sun came out. Jacob had finished the mowing by then and the lawns looked amazing. Daddy was sad about all the wildflowers we'd lost, but we could now see there were lots of other flowers in the beds. Roses, foxgloves, alliums, some white ones we didn't recognise.

After lunch we got back to it. Jacob tidied up the beds with Mr Coleman's strimmer. There wasn't time to weed them all properly, but they looked so much better with a trim. Vicky tidied up Mummy's veggie patch, which had been looking a little neglected since Mummy hadn't been there to look after it. She found some tomatoes, runner beans and a couple of massive courgettes. Emily, Daisy, Tamsin and I scrubbed and swept and wiped and polished the summerhouse. Now all it needed were some finishing touches.

We went into the house and up into the loft, tiptoeing in so as to not wake the bats. Up there was a treasure trove of old furniture. We took some wooden chairs and a small table, and Daddy and Jacob carried a dusty old armchair with some holes in the upholstery. We took all this out to the summerhouse. Vicky quickly made up some little curtains for the windows and the glass panels on the doors from scraps of fabric at her house. Tamsin and Daisy found loads of candles and put some on the windowsill and some on the table. Finally, we took some of the wildflowers we'd cut and made big, fancy displays with them.

We stepped back and surveyed our work. It looked fantastic, but . . .

'There's something missing,' Vicky said.

'What?' I asked.

'Wait here,' she said and walked off across the neat lawn. Five minutes later she came back carrying a big bundle of something.

'What's that?' Daisy asked.

'I know exactly what it is,' I said. 'Bunting!'

'I might just cut one more branch off that rhododendron,' Daddy said. 'The leaves are still brushing the roof.'

While we hung up the bunting, Daddy started sawing the branch. It was a really big one and took him ages. As we were putting up the last bit, we heard a cry. We rushed outside to find Daddy on his knees, one hand on his side.

'My back,' he said. 'I've done my back in.'

We had to help him into the summerhouse and settle him down on the armchair. Jacob went and got a box of matches and we lit all the candles. Not because it was dark, but just to see how it would look. Some of the candles were aromatherapy candles and they smelled amazing, masking the faint scent of the creosote. It was so peaceful there. A perfect retreat for Mummy.

'I'll plant some honeysuckle to climb up the walls,' Daddy said.

'Not honeysuckle,' I said. 'Clematis.'

'OK,' he agreed, grinning, then winced with the pain in his back.

Despite the injury to Daddy, the last night before Mummy returned was a very happy occasion. We decided we were going to eat in the summerhouse. Vicky discovered all the eggs and made us huge omelettes, and a cheese and hummus sandwich for William D. It was lovely to sit there and drink lemonade and look back at the house and at the garden, so pretty now. Mummy will be thrilled, I thought.

'The only thing we didn't get time to do was the rhododendron at the side,' Daddy said. 'Oh well.' He winced again with the pain and shifted uncomfortably on his chair. 'I'm sure Mummy will be happy with what we've done. She'll understand.'

I wasn't so sure. I think, on the whole, it would have been better if we'd started with the rhododendron instead of leaving it until last. But now didn't seem the time to mention it, not after all the work we'd got done today.

'I'll get you another cushion,' I said, getting up. But I got up too quickly and bumped the table. One of the candles, in a tall wine bottle, wobbled slowly. It looked like it might fall over the side. Daddy's eyes widened in alarm. He tried to stand but his back seized up and he froze.

'Catch it, Chloe!' he shouted. The bottle tipped and for a moment it looked like it might wobble back, but then it carried on, in slow-motion. It was going to fall! I leaned across the table to try to grab it. But it was too far and I lost my balance and fell face first into the salad. My outstretched hand closed on thin air, a few centimetres short of the bottle, which, as I watched, went slowly over the edge and went down, out of sight.

Straight away there was a WHOOF! sound and flames shot up from where the candle had fallen.

'The creosote!' Daddy said. Jacob reacted quickly and pulled the table back away from the flames. Daddy was right. The candle had fallen right into the open tin of creosote, and already flames were shooting up high, licking the bunting. Jacob darted forward to grab the tin but Daddy grabbed him and held him back.

'Too dangerous,' he said. 'Everyone out, now!'

We all got outside. My heart was pounding. Turning around, we saw the bunting had now caught fire and the flames were tickling the ceiling.

'No!' I shouted. Mummy's retreat was being destroyed before our eyes.

'Yeaaahhhhh!' William D shrieked. He was the only one enjoying it.

'My bunting!' Vicky Bellamy said, hands on cheeks.

'My candles!' Daisy said.

'My back,' Daddy said, bending over like an old man.

'It's all my fault,' I cried.

'No, it's not,' Daddy said. 'I left the tin of creosote out with no lid. It's my fault.'

But it *was* my fault. I felt the tears welling up and they just wouldn't stop. Daddy hobbled over and gave me a hug.

'Hey,' he said. 'It doesn't matter. It's only an old shed. The important thing is that you're safe. We're all safe.'

'But we worked so hard on it,' I said. 'All of us. Finally there was one part of the house that was just perfect. And this was my Big Plan and when Mummy got back we were all going to be together and she'd be happy.'

Daddy groaned as he went down on his knees so he could look into my face. 'Chloe, sweetheart. I know the house isn't perfect,' he said. 'And I know I'm not perfect either. None of us are. But it's OK to not be perfect. It's OK to be a bit rambling and messy. And believe me, Mummy is happy, even if she gets cross sometimes. She loves you madly. And she loves Daisy and William D and Jacob and she loves me and she loves our house too. Despite everything.'

I hugged him tightly even though I could feel him wincing because of his back.

'What on earth is going on now?' yelled a new voice. Mr Coleman had popped his head over the fence.

'Just a little creosote fire,' Daddy said calmly as the roof suddenly burst into flames, the black sticky stuff crackling like fireworks on Bonfire Night. He got to his feet gingerly. 'Nothing to worry about.'

'"Nothing to worry about"!' Mr Coleman spluttered. 'There are garages on the other side of your back fence. If they go up who knows what damage the fire will cause? I'm phoning the fire brigade.'

'Probably a good idea,' Daddy said, as one of the curtains burst into flames. I could see a single blue aromatherapy candle in the midst of the blaze; the fire hadn't got to it yet and it was still burning peacefully, giving off its scent. Tears rolled down my face and I felt Daisy's hand creep into mine.

'It's getting hotter,' I said.

'Hotter than Marmite,' Daisy muttered.

Before I knew it, I heard sirens in York Road. Emily pulled me away to the side to watch as an enormous fireman came down the side of the house. When he saw the rhododendron blocking the path he grabbed a huge axe and demolished it in a few strokes, leaving thick, black branches lying like severed limbs. Then he and another firefighter charged through, pulling a thick hose with them.

William D was in heaven. Fires, fire engines, axes, hoses. He'd remember this day for a long time, that was for sure. The firefighters put the fire out very quickly and then spoke to Daddy about taking more care with flammable substances. As they were leaving, William D ran up for a closer look. One of the firefighters stopped. I recognised her as the lady firefighter we'd seen at the School Fair. She knelt down to speak to him.

'I remember you,' she said. 'You're the little chap who reset the computer on the engine.'

'Yes, that was me,' William D replied. 'Happy to help.'

'It's never been the same since, that computer,' she said.

'He's inherited his computer skills from me, I'm afraid,' Daddy said.

The firefighter winked and stood to go. As she passed down the side of the house she moved aside to let someone else through.

'Thanks,' said a familiar voice.

'MUMMY!' William D cried and ran into her arms. Daisy and I were right behind him and we ran so hard into her she fell over.

'I've missed you all so much,' Mummy said.

'We've missed you too,' I said. 'You're back early!'

'Is everyone OK?' Mummy asked. 'Why is the fire brigade here?'

'We made you a retreat and it had cushions and candles and creosote but it burned down and it's all my fault,' I said quickly, the words rushing into one another.

'A retreat? What are you talking about?'

So we took her down to the bottom of the garden to see the smoking ruins of the summerhouse in the twilight. Daddy was sitting in a singed armchair that the firefighters had pulled out of the burning summerhouse. He waved.

'You could get up,' Mummy said.

'No, I couldn't,' replied Daddy.

Our House

Mummy got us all inside and said goodbye to Vicky, who took Tamsin and Emily home. She got us undressed and threw our smoky clothes into the washing machine. We all had a bath together like when we were tiny and Mummy told us about the retreat.

'It was grim,' she said. 'There's a reason people like to cook their vegetables. And if I never see another cup of herbal flipping tea it'll be too soon.'

'What were the other people like?' Daisy asked.

'Awful. Far too *limber*,' Mummy said. 'They just kept smiling and flopping about doing yoga and relaxation exercises. That's why I came back early, I couldn't stand it any longer.'

'Sorry about the fire brigade being here when you got back,' I said. 'That probably wasn't very relaxing.'

'No, perhaps not,' Mummy said. Then she got us out and helped us into our pyjamas and we all went downstairs and snuggled up between Mummy and Daddy on the sofa.

When I was tucked up later that night, Mummy sat on the side of my bed and smiled at me.

'I missed you,' I said.

'I missed you too,' she said, brushing hair away from my face.

'Do you think you might need to go away again?' I asked.

'No. I think I made a mistake leaving you all. I won't be doing it again.'

'But you needed your retreat,' I said.

'Oh, sweetie,' she said. 'I hated every minute of it. I wanted to come back as soon as I got there.'

'Why didn't you?' I asked.

'Because I paid up front,' Mummy said. 'I'm joking. I suppose I thought it was good for you all if I was away for a few days. Your daddy needed to spend some time with you without me. But I felt so guilty, Chloe. I won't be doing it again.'

'What if you start to feel trapped again?' I asked.

'Ah, but that's not going to happen,' she said. 'Not any more.'

'How do you know?' I asked.

'Because now the rhododendron's been cut down, I can come and go as I please,' she explained. 'I have my emergency exit. Who needs a front door that opens? Not me.'

I reached up and gave her a hug. She squeezed me tight.

'Daddy told me you talked to him about what's been going on at school,' she said. 'About Imogen being mean to you, and you being worried about your party.'

I nodded. 'I didn't want you to be upset,' I said.

Mummy wiped her eye. 'I don't want you to ever feel you can't talk to me about what's worrying you,' she said. 'I've been such a terrible mummy, not noticing what you were going through.'

'It's OK,' I said. I felt a bit embarrassed about what Mummy was saying. Despite all my efforts, she felt bad.

'It's not OK,' Mummy said. 'I want you to tell me these things. In return I promise I'll listen and I won't be upset and we'll work through our problems together, yes?'

'Yes,' I said, smiling. 'Mummy?'

'Yes, sweetie?'

'Can we have a party? Now we've sorted out the garden?' I asked. 'Not just for me. But for all of us. For the house too.'

Mummy hesitated for a moment, but then nodded. 'Of course we can. I'll get on the phone tomorrow and start thinking about food and maybe I can borrow Mrs Groves' trestle tables and . . .'

'Can we do it together?' I asked. 'All of us? Because this is a party for you too and you shouldn't have to do everything.'

She paused for a bit before nodding. 'I'd like that,' she said. 'We'll call it a late birthday party and a very late housewarming.'

'Thanks, Mummy,' I said.

'Now it's late,' she said. 'You need to get to sleep.' She kissed me, stood and walked to the door.

'Mummy,' I said, as she was leaving. She stopped and looked back at me. 'I dreamed you came back one night and tucked me in.'

'Sweetie,' she said. 'I came back a few times. I even stayed in the spare room one night.'

'What? Really?'

'Yes. Who do you think did the washing? Who bought the food?'

'That was you? We thought it was a ghost. Or Jacob. But more likely a ghost.'

She laughed.

'Did Daddy know?'

'No. I didn't tell him and he didn't notice. He's not very observant, your father. I could see you and Daddy were all getting on just fine, apart from the washing and the food. I just wanted to make sure you were OK. You *were* OK, weren't you?'

I nodded. 'We had fun.'

'Good,' she said. Then she turned off the light. 'Night night, sweetie.'

'Night night, Mummy.'

But before I went to sleep, I got up and crossed to my window seat, where the copy of my report was. There was something I wanted to change. I looked at the front page, at the title.

My House

I took a thick marker pen and wrote:

Our ~~My~~ House

Saturday

The next morning, I got up when Daddy got up, which was when William D got up, which was very early. Daddy was a bit surprised to see me. He stood in his dressing gown, hair all messy, propped up against the Aga and yawned at me.

'Why are you up so early?' he asked.

'It's part of my Big Plan,' I said. 'Where do we keep the string?'

So when Mummy woke up, she found a piece of string at the end of her bed with a note saying 'FOLLOW THE STRING.' The string first led her upstairs to my room. Daddy and I followed her. She went in and on the bed was the first part of my report. The part about my room.

'Read it,' I said. She smiled and took the report. Mummy sat on my bed and started to read. When she finished she looked up at me.

'Chloe, this is lovely,' she said.

'There's more,' I said, hopping from foot to foot. 'Keep following the string.'

It led her to the spare room next, then to Jacob's room, then back down to William D's room, then downstairs to the living room, then to Front Door, then the kitchen, then out into the garden.

And in every room she went into there was a section of my school project waiting for her. She sat and read each one in turn while we peeked around the door. She smiled a lot, and laughed sometimes, and she had a little cry at one point but Daddy said that was a good thing.

When she'd read the last bit, the bit about the garden, she came and gave me a big hug.

'I love you, Chloe,' she said. 'I love all of you, and I love this house too. You've put into words better than I ever could how happy I am. I know I grumble about the flappy wallpaper and the electrics and the groaning radiators. And I know I get cross with you sometimes. None of us are perfect and neither is the house.'

'This is the perfect house for us,' I said.

'It is,' she said. 'And we're the perfect family for it.'

Emergency Exit

After breakfast Mummy spent a lot of time walking up and down the side path where the rhododendron had been. She had a big grin on her face.

'So much space,' she kept saying. Then suddenly, as I watched, she stopped and peered at something on the ground. She bent down and reached deep into what was left of the bush, pulled out a sheaf of papers and looked at them.

I walked up to see what she was looking at.

'Notes from William D's school,' she said, showing me. 'That little monkey. I should have known . . .'

'He's been stashing them all here,' I said.

'I thought it was suspicious that we hadn't had any notes AT ALL since we started the star chart,' Mummy said. 'He's a cunning little beast.'

'Not that cunning,' I said. 'Or he'd have realised he'd get found out when the rhododendron was cut down.'

'If it wasn't for the fire the rhododendron would NEVER have been cut down,' Mummy pointed out. 'He must have realised this was the safest place of all.'

'Are you going to take his Pokémon away?' I asked.

Mummy thought about it for a while but then shook her head.

'No, he deserves it as a reward for sheer cunning. I'll have to try a different approach next time.'

NEXT Saturday

It was the day of the big party. I'd told my friends it was for my birthday but really it was for all of us. I woke up late in a bit of a panic because I was supposed to be up and helping. I rushed to the window and was pleased to see the day was sunny and already starting to feel warm. Mummy said lots of people had accepted the invitation but she wouldn't say who. I was a bit worried. When I got downstairs, Emily was sitting at our kitchen table eating cereal with Daisy. I saw Mummy, Daddy, Jacob and Vicky were already out in the garden getting things ready. There were picnic tables laid out in a line, there was a bouncy castle, there was a BBQ all set up and Jacob was arranging his turntable and speakers for the music. Vicky Bellamy was putting up bunting, of course. It hadn't taken her long at all to replace the lengths that had been burned.

At the end of the garden was a big marquee, where the summerhouse had been.

'I thought you said we didn't have a marquee,' I said to Mummy.

'We didn't,' she said. 'But after poor old Imogen's

party was ruined I thought it might be a good idea to get one.'

The party started at midday and people started arriving soon after that. Funnily enough, Front Door worked fine today. Daddy said it was because it was a dry day. Mummy said it was because Front Door knew the rhododendron was gone so there was no point playing silly games any more. Daisy said it was because Front Door was happy we were having a party and was in a welcoming mood.

'I think Daisy's right,' I said. 'After all, this party isn't just for the family, it's for the whole house, even Front Door.'

Mr Coleman was the first to come. Mummy whispered to me that she'd had to invite him so he wouldn't complain about the noise later on. Mr and Mrs Guptil came too. They're lovely and Mr Guptil gave me an envelope with some money in it that Mummy took and said would be going into my trust fund, as soon as she'd set one up for me.

Our neighbours-from-the-other-way, Justin and Gavin, came too. They're really nice and very funny. They said their favourite time of the day is when they hear Mummy out the back of our house saying 'DOOBY-DOOBY-DOO!!'

Next to arrive was Cara. I had to introduce her to Daddy as he'd never been up early enough to see her.

'She's a great help, and lovely company,' Cara said to them.

'Is she? Err . . . yes, she is, I suppose,' Daddy said, confused. I'd never quite got around to telling my parents about Cara. I ushered her away and introduced her to Justin and Gavin. They didn't have milk delivered and so wouldn't give me away and also I thought Cara might want to try to sign them up.

I felt a tap on my shoulder. It was Mummy with an old man I didn't recognise.

'This is Mr Simpson, Chloe,' Mummy said. My jaw dropped before I remembered my manners.

'Pleased to meet you,' I said. He looked in excellent health. 'Where's Mrs Simpson?'

'She's not feeling very well,' Mr Simpson said. 'I don't think she'll be joining us.'

It was a huge relief to meet Mr Simpson and to know he was OK. Though now I was slightly concerned about Mrs Simpson. It wasn't like her to be ill. It was nice to have lots of the neighbours around, and Emily. But I was hoping some more of my friends might come. I shouldn't have worried though, because soon we heard more people coming around the side of the house. It was Hannah and Sophie, who seemed delighted to be there. They gave me presents and a big hug.

'I've never been to your house, Chloe,' Sophie said. 'I love your garden!'

I blushed. It's true our house isn't as big or fancy as a lot of the houses around here. But our garden is bigger and better than just about anyone's I know, especially now it's been tidied up. The cherry tree is fruiting, and the damsons are starting to go purple. We'd found an apple tree we hadn't even known about. There's so much space to run around now.

Then Oliver and Thomas arrived. Oliver was carrying a football and after saying a quick happy birthday and shoving a present into my hands he ran off to play on lawn two, where there was more space. Thomas stayed for a moment longer. He looked really nervous, then he handed me the present and thanked his shoes for inviting him to the party. Then he ran off after Oliver.

'He likes you!' Hannah said.

'Shut up!' I said, feeling my face go red. I looked down at the present he'd given me. The paper was a pattern of book spines in an old bookshop. Thomas knew I liked books. I wondered if he'd chosen the paper himself.

Gurinder and Ellie turned up next, then Tamsin. Then Georgie Turner who was my best friend in London and I haven't seen for ages. Then Tobias, who can be a bit of a handful at parties but is always very enthusiastic. His mummy stayed to help out. There was still one person who was invited who hadn't turned up. I kept looking towards the Emergency Exit hoping she'd come as the afternoon went on. We had a barbecue and ate cake, then played a massive game of BOOMball, all together. Mr Guptil was hit on the head but he seemed to enjoy it. Mr Coleman shook his head and went off to sit in the marquee with a glass of wine. After that DJ

Deal started up and the grown-ups sat together and chatted and we all jumped about to Katy Perry and Little Mix. Even the boys joined in. Tobias burned off lots of energy.

As I jumped and spun I suddenly saw the last guest arrive. It was Charlie. I ran over to her.

'Thanks for coming,' I said.

'Thanks for inviting me,' she replied. 'Sorry I'm late. My shift ran over.' She handed me a present. Charlie looked very pretty. She had make-up on but you had to really look to notice. But as I leaned forward to take the present from her I smelled a little hint of vinegar. My heart sank. She hadn't got the message!

'Jacob's on the tables,' I told her.

'I've come to see you,' Charlie said. 'Not Jacob.'

I must have looked disappointed.

'Chloe, I work in a chip shop. I'm Chip Shop Charlie. I smell of vinegar,' she said. 'And if that puts Jacob off, then so be it. I'm not going to go home and scrub my skin every night just for a boy. Even if he is a rather gorgeous boy with two lovely sisters.'

'And a brother,' Daisy reminded her. 'Don't forget William D.'

'How could I forget William D?' Charlie asked. We turned to watch him race through a crowd of people, carrying the football and chased by a furious Oliver and Thomas.

Charlie came and danced with us for a while and I

saw Jacob pretending not to watch her. During a song, Hannah's phone went off and it was Imogen on Facetime, phoning from Barbados. We all clustered around the screen to see how she was getting on. She looked grumpy.

'It's raining here,' she said. 'We can't go to the beach. Where are you?'

'We're at Chloe's party,' Hannah shouted over the music. 'It's the best!'

'Who's there?' Imogen asked. Now she looked even more grumpy.

'Everyone,' Hannah said.

Everyone who matters, I thought. I looked around at my family, my friends, my little world. I saw Emily leaping about with Daisy and Tamsin. I saw Charlie, now standing next to Jacob on the turntables; he was showing her how to work the controls and she was laughing. I saw Thomas and Oliver shrieking and leaping; I saw Vicky and Mr Simpson and Mr Coleman and Mr and Mrs Guptil and Justin and Gavin. I saw Daddy laughing at something Mummy had said. Laughing so hard he couldn't breathe.

I put my arm around Hannah and peered at Imogen's furious face on the little screen.

'I'm really sorry to hear it's raining in Barbados, Imogen,' I said. 'Really, *really* sorry.'

Now THAT'S sarcasm.

And so the music blared and we danced under the sun in the garden at the back of our house. As the light eventually faded Jacob suddenly brought the volume right down. We looked over at him and he pointed up into the sky. Craning our necks we saw hundreds of tiny black shapes streaming silently from somewhere under the eaves and heading out into the dusk. Slowly, getting louder and louder, Jacob mixed a new track into the old one. It took me a moment before I recognised it.

It was the *Batman* theme tune. Suddenly William D was there on the picnic table, fists raised into the air triumphantly, screaming at the top of his lungs.

'AW-KWAAARD!'

Shouty Dad

A couple of days later, I was reading in my room when I heard a very familiar, and very loud, voice out in the street.

'OK, TURN IT ON NOW!'

'Daisy, Daisy!' I shouted and rushed to the window.

Daisy came running in, her face lit up like a plasma screen. We knelt together on the window seat and stuck our heads out into the bright sunshine. There, on the driveway of the Dukes' house over the road, stood Shouty Dad, triumphantly returned and shoutier than ever.

'He's back!' Daisy cried with delight. I grinned at her and nodded.

'IS IT ON?!' he screamed back towards the house. 'IT'S NOT WORKING!'

He was holding a hose. The two girls were at the side of the house, messing about with the outside tap.

'THERE'S PROBABLY A KINK!' he shouted. 'TRY AND STRAIGHTEN THE HOSE.'

He waited for a while but nothing happened. One of the girls called something back to him and he pointed the nozzle of the hose up to peer into it. Quickly one of

279

the girls straightened a kink in the hose and it emitted a powerful jet of water right into Shouty Dad's face, soaking him instantly.

'AAARGH!' he yelled. 'FOR THE LOVE OF . . . HOW DID THAT HAPPEN?'

An upstairs window opened and Mrs Duke stuck her head out. She must have said something to Mr Duke because he stopped and looked up at her.

'I'LL DO THAT IN A MINUTE!' he screamed in response. 'FOR HEAVEN'S SAKE, I'M TRYING TO WATER THE FRONT GARDEN. IT'S PARCHED. PARCHED!'

Daisy and I smiled at each other. Everything was back where it should be.

Look out for the next brilliant
OUR HOUSE story . . .

Life is never simple for the Deal family . . .
Imogen is being unbearable in the school play,
and has a kissing scene with Thomas! Daddy's job
means he is working abroad while Mummy
re-decorates the house, and the builders are
causing nearly as much chaos as William D. Will
OUR HOUSE ever shine and sparkle?

Piccadilly
PRESS

Thank you for choosing a Piccadilly Press book.

If you would like to know more about our
authors, our books or if you'd just like to know
what we're up to, you can find us online.

www.piccadillypress.co.uk

You can also find us on:

We hope to see you soon!